THE SECRETS
OF
STONEWOOD
SANITARIUM

LINDA A. KRUG

Outskirts Press, Inc.
Denver, Colorado

Cover Photo © 2009 JupiterImages Corporation. All rights reserved - used with permission.

Outskirts Press, Inc.
http://www.outskirtspress.com

ISBN: 978-1-4327-2981-3

Library of Congress Control Number: 2009922817

Outskirts Press and the "OP" logo are trademarks belonging to Outskirts Press, Inc.

PRINTED IN THE UNITED STATES OF AMERICA

DEDICATION

This book is dedicated to Steven and Mary Krug. Not a day goes by that I don't think of you and realize how fortunate I was to have you as parents. Thank you for making me the strong, independent, and fearless person whose reflection I see in the mirror. May you continue to rest in peace. You are loved and missed -- more than words could ever say.

CHAPTER 1

In the darkness, a wild animal howled, and the moon emerged from behind the clouds. A boy sat up in his makeshift bed, reaching over to shake his sleeping brother's arm.

"Eric! Eric!" he whispered urgently. "It's time."

Not waiting for his brother to fully awaken, the boy retrieved two torches from the corner of the room. They would need them in the tunnel, where the moon's light did not reach. The embers from a small fire still glowed in the center of the room, and the boy lit the torches and handed one to his brother. Together they made their way into the tunnel. They were joined by others, and the group cautiously made their way down the passageway, careful to avoid the stream running down the center of the escape route and the tree roots dangling from the crumbling ceiling. When the group neared the end of the passage, they extinguished their lights and emerged into the open.

"Head for the bushes," the boy commanded in a low voice. "We don't want to be seen."

They slipped into a dense thicket, inching forward as soundlessly as they could, occasionally glancing up at the stars for direction.

"Stop!"

The group froze.

"Stop right there, you dirty heathens! Stop, before I shoot!"

"Run!" the boy screamed. "Keep together and run!"

A series of pops, like firecrackers, punctuated the air, and suddenly his brother fell to the ground. The boy dropped to his knees and pressed his hand over the spurting wound in his brother's neck.

His brother's eyes widened, and his lips moved, shaping the words, "Make it. Make it to freedom."

"We will," the boy promised, as tears streamed down his face. "For you and the others that couldn't."

His brother smiled his last smile and died in his arms.

"Eric!" yelled Nate. He suddenly realized he was sitting on a bus, and all the other passengers had turned around in their seats and were staring at him.

An elderly gentleman crossed the aisle and laid his hand on Nate's shoulder.

"Son, that must have been one whopper of a dream. Are you okay?"

"Yeah. I think so. Th-thanks for asking," replied Nate, willing his heart to slow down. "I'm all right."

"Would you like a soda? I have an extra one."

"No, thanks. I'll be okay. Really I will."

"Well, if you need me I'll be over there," the man said, pointing and then returning to his seat.

Glancing out the window, Nate discovered he'd awakened just in time to see the sign welcoming him to Forest County, Pennsylvania.

Nate Thompson had been on and off buses for thirteen hours, crossing from New Jersey into New York and then across Pennsylvania. Now, a few miles from his destination, he pulled a worn newspaper clipping from his shirt pocket and gently unfolded it, careful to avoid tearing it any more than he already had. Reading and rereading the article had become a bad habit, one he wished he could break. The bold print of the featured story never failed to send a chill down his spine.

LOCAL SCIENTIST, WIFE, AND SON
PERISH IN AIRPLANE CRASH

Nate looked up from the article and stared out the bus window. He would have been on that plane with his parents and older brother if it hadn't been for baseball camp. Nate remembered how he'd bugged his parents unmercifully to attend. At first reluctant -- his family wanted him to accompany them on their once-in-a-lifetime trip to Brazil -- they caved in with one condition. He'd be responsible for half of the registration fee.

"Money doesn't grow on trees. You're fourteen now, and you've got to learn the meaning of a dollar," his father had said.

Nate never complained about the odd jobs he did to earn that money; he saw it as a challenge he knew he could meet, and he did.

He said good-bye to his parents and brother that third weekend in June. Dad rubbed Nate's head. Mom, as usual cried, sobbing she was going to miss her little man. Eric, Nate's only sibling, said his good-byes in the usual way. "Take it easy, turd. Don't break any bones or takes hits to your head. You're already brain-damaged as it is."

Nate returned the farewell.

"Thanks, puke-breath. Have a nice time in Brazil. Hope you

drink contaminated water and get the runs."

"Sure thing, loser. Wish the same for you," responded Eric.

"I'm counting on a tsetse fly biting you, so you can heave up your guts the whole way home."

"If I do, I'll save the big chunks for you."

"And I'll --" Nate began. He was abruptly interrupted by his dad.

"Boys, knock it off! Zip it! If you don't have anything nice to say to each other, don't say anything at all."

Nate and Eric grinned at one another. They knew it was just their unique way of bidding each other adieu.

Now, less than a month later, Nate was on a bus heading toward his new home, a tiny village in northwestern Pennsylvania where his Uncle Nick and Aunt Nora lived. They were supposed to become his new parents, but as much as he loved them, there was no way they could do that. He unzipped a side pocket in his backpack, pushed his electronic game aside, and pulled out a framed family picture. Mom, Dad, Eric, and Nate -- the all-American family, living the all-American dream. Nate remembered telling his mother that baseball camp lasted only a week. They'd be back together in no time.

He clutched their picture to his chest as tears filled his eyes. He didn't care how sissy it looked. He wanted fights with his brother, table-manner lectures, and "clean your room" details back. He wouldn't even mind escaping from a subterranean tunnel -- just as long as he could do it with Eric, and nobody had to die.

But that was not the way life worked. Nate's mother always told him never to question the will of God. "He knows what He's doing even if we humans don't have a clue," she'd say.

He found comfort in that thought. With the back of his hand, Nate wiped the tears from his face. No amount of sobbing or bargaining with God was going to bring his family back. They were gone. No matter how brokenhearted he was, he needed to move on with the rest of his life. He'd honor their memory by being the type of person they would have wanted him to be. He just didn't know exactly how.

In the pocket of his backpack where the picture had been, Nate spotted a book on Forest County that his Aunt Nora had sent him. He pulled it out and flipped to the chapter describing his new hometown. It would sure be different from the suburbs of northern New Jersey. He had lived in Madison his entire life. His home had been minutes away from everything -- the supermarket, school, mall, and ball parks. This place where his aunt and uncle lived was in the middle of nowhere -- he and Eric had always jokingly called it "Snoozeville."

He picked up the catcher's mitt and slipped his hand into it, smiling at the comfortable way it fit his hand. He would make the best of his new situation. He'd give his new surroundings a fair chance. He had no other choice. He was leaving his suburban life in Madison, New Jersey to start anew in Woodson, Pennsylvania -- and his new life started today.

CHAPTER 2

"Nathan!" Aunt Nora cried.

Alighting from the bus with his backpack over his shoulders, Nate followed the sound of her voice. There she was, chubby and jovial, waving frantically at the edge of the platform. Next to her stood Nick, her husband, his massive Paul Bunyan arms crossed over his chest. Cheered by the mere sight of his mother's older sister, Nate flew straight into her arms.

"Darling, how was your trip? I wish you'd come home with us right after the memorial service," said his Aunt Nora.

"I appreciated the offer. I just needed some alone time. Time to think things through and put them in perspective."

"I know," said Nora, kissing Nate's curly brown hair.

Uncle Nick tapped the backpack. "This all the luggage you brought, sport?"

"Oh, sorry, no." Nate extricated himself from Aunt Nora's clutches and retrieved his other two suitcases from the bay beneath the bus.

"Let me," Uncle Nick said, and picked up the heaviest suitcase as if it were a pillow with a handle on the side. Nate resigned himself to be cuddled by Aunt Nora, and they headed off for the Bluemobile, Uncle Nick's beloved 1967 Ford pickup.

Nick and Nora lived on a thirty-acre organic farm on German Hill Road, three miles east of Woodson. Their property was a mixture of sprawling meadows, woods, and plowed fields. It was picture-postcard pretty. Uncle Nick worked the land and Aunt Nora managed the books. They had no children of their own, but Nate knew he'd be in good hands.

Nate had always enjoyed his country vacations. His Uncle Nick was a man's man and liked doing "guy" things. He fished, hunted, four-wheeled, and crushed beer cans on his head. It was Nick who taught Nate the art of lassoing. About a quarter of a mile from the farmhouse, Uncle Nick built an obstacle course equipped with a rope ladder, a scaling wall, an inner tube, and sections of barbed wire. A decorated Vietnam veteran, Uncle Nick was convinced that America needed to be ready to fight off foreign invaders -- and he didn't always mean terrorists.

Uncle Nick loved to tell war stories, and when he wasn't getting teary-eyed remembering fallen comrades, he'd tell of alien encounters. He was convinced there were extraterrestrials living around the world who were conspiring to take over Earth. Nate knew his uncle wasn't a crackpot, just a good guy who wanted to protect his home and family from any and all threats.

Nate had remembered from previous visits that the area was very rural, but now, looking out the window, he realized it was possible to look for miles into the distance without seeing a single commercial building.

7

"Uncle Nick, does everybody around here farm?"

Uncle Nick laughed. "Seems like it, doesn't it? No, there are a few people in Forest County who punch a clock. The two biggest employers, believe it or not, are the Department of Corrections and the state hospital. The state of Pennsylvania built a prison up here a few years ago. They house 2,500 inmates over at Oakdale, where we picked you up. Poor yahoos -- I feel sorry if one of those convicts escape. They wear brown jumpsuits and could easily be mistaken for a bear. Lots of those clowns are from the city and don't know the first thing about surviving in these woods -- and if nature doesn't kill them, the locals might. Some people will shoot at anything up here. Shoot first, look second, and ask questions third. Yeah, I feel sorry for the first sap that tries an escape attempt. They'll have to transport him to the hospital to get the buckshot out of his rear end!"

It happened so suddenly, it caught Nate off guard. He'd had this happen before -- a fear so primal that it felt like ice water running down his back. He gasped for breath as the chill penetrated him, and the hair on the back of his neck stood up.

"Uncle Nick, are we by a river or pond? I just got a big chill," Nate said.

"No, son. No lakes or rivers along this stretch of road. Just passing the state hospital and the old sanitarium. They're over on your right."

Nate frowned. "Sanitarium?"

"Used to be the nut house before they built the new one. You know, where they keep the nuts. Walnuts, hazelnuts, peanuts, Brazil nuts."

"Nick, that's enough," Aunt Nora said abruptly. "You know I don't like it when you refer to those poor people that way."

"What do you mean? Coconuts, almonds --"

Aunt Nora turned toward Nate. "Honey, what Uncle Nick is trying to say is we're passing the state psychiatric hospital, where mentally-ill individuals live."

"Yeah, the looney-toons," continued Uncle Nick, taking his right hand off the steering wheel and making circular motions by the side of his head. "The certifiably insane."

"Then why aren't you living there?" Aunt Nora asked her husband.

"Not enough room. But it was sweet of you to take me in," he said, blowing a kiss in her direction.

"Lucky me," she replied.

Then she turned toward Nate. "Sweetie, you need to stay away from those places. The grounds are divided into two sections. The new hospital is called Forest State Hospital. The old hospital was called Stonewood Sanitarium. The new hospital is operational and has patients. They don't use the old side anymore. They attached the new hospital to the old so they could hook into the same underground sewer and water lines, but no one sets foot in the old portion. It's been condemned. That whole section is supposed to be boarded up and padlocked, but you know how that goes."

"Is there any way you can get to the old hospital from the new one?" Nate asked.

"There's not supposed to be. They sealed all the entrances and erected wire fencing around most of it. They didn't want the patients from the new hospital wandering over to the old section."

She was interrupted by Uncle Nick.

"No kidding, Nate, it really is dangerous. Last year two trespassers were crushed by chunks of the old building falling on them. Some kind of investigative reporters from Pittsburgh. Nobody knows what they were doing snooping around the old hospital. By the time they were found, they'd been on the grounds for about a week, enough time for the wolves and bobcats to feed on them. Strange thing, though, is that they just found the bodies -- no notebooks, briefcases, cell phones -- none of the stuff reporters should have on them. And I don't think bobcats eat cell phones!"

"Who found them?" Nate asked.

"Nelson. Superintendent Nelson. He's the director of the new hospital. He's been running the place for the last five years. Runs a real tight ship, too."

"What do you mean by that?" Nate asked.

"You see him over there days, nights, and weekends, prowling the sanitarium's grounds. Stays right on top of things, and if for some reason he's not there himself, somebody on his staff patrols the perimeter -- if you can call two officers a staff. Marvin and that big ugly fellow. Honey, what's his name? The one that looks like Lurch?"

"I don't know," Aunt Nora said, sounding annoyed. She turned her attention back to Nate.

"Honey, horrific things went on inside that old hospital when it was in operation. Terrible, horrendous things. I can't bring myself to talk about it. It would offend anyone that has an ounce of morality or dignity. So even though Superintendent Nelson and his men are doing their best to keep everyone safe, it's not a good place for anyone to roam around in, especially a youngster. I don't want you going there."

"Yeah, Nate, listen up," Uncle Nick continued. "Every now and then you'll have a patient walking away from the new hospital. The less dangerous ones, the more stable nuts --"

"Nicky, what did you say?" Aunt Nora interrupted.

"Sorry, Nora. The more stable patients," he corrected pointedly, "have extra privileges. They aren't locked down like the dangerous ones. Anyway, every now and then one of them wanders off hospital grounds. The staff, with help from the county sheriffs and state police, usually locates them along the road. The -- *escapees* -- don't give anyone a problem. They're loaded in a vehicle and taken back to the hospital."

"When did the last one wander off?" Nate asked.

"Couple of years. Two or three," he replied, turning to Nora for confirmation.

She nodded her head in agreement. "Nathan, honey, if you're ever confronted by one of them, remain calm. Don't excite them. Act as if everything is normal. Get one of us and we'll deal with the situation. Okay?"

Nate nodded his head.

"That's right, son." Uncle Nick took over the conversation. "They don't mean any harm. Most of them are medicated and walk around like -- what do they call the dead people in the movies who walk around looking for the living so they can eat their brains?"

"Zombies," Nate supplied.

"Yeah, zombies. The walking dead," replied his uncle.

"Nick, you're getting on my last nerve," said Aunt Nora darkly.

"Sorry, babe. But Nate, you get my drift. They walk around like they're in trances -- like they're sleepwalking, but without holding their arms out in front of them. Know what I mean?"

"Honey, ignore him. He's a zombie," Aunt Nora said. "But seriously, sweetie, people have told me there are underground coal shafts and sinkholes around the old hospital. One false move and you could fall in. You'd never be heard from again."

"Nora, for Pete's sake. The boy doesn't know what a sinkhole is."

"Yes, I do," Nate said eagerly. "It's an opening in the ground. They form when underground material dissolves or collapses."

Nick looked impressed. "Nora, we have a genius in our family.

Most adults couldn't explain that as well as Nate."

Nate smiled, feeling kind of proud. Science club was finally paying off.

"Nathan, honey, you do promise us that you'll stay away from both hospitals?"

"Okay," Nate said, nodding his head in agreement. "I'll try," he added in a lower voice. Right now, those two hospitals sounded like the most interesting things in Woodson.

Uncle Nick pulled into the driveway and started unloading Nate's luggage. They were greeted by Max, the family's border collie, and Izzie, their pet goat. Uncle Nick patted Izzie's head.

"Won't be long. She's due any day. Good girl," he said gently, rubbing her ears.

Nate had never been able to have animals due to Dad's allergies, but he had always wanted a pet. He knelt down to hug Max and Izzie and reintroduce himself. His meeting was interrupted by a squalling crow that landed on a nearby fencepost. It created a ruckus no one could ignore. Nate stood up and walked toward the feathered creature. The bird let him get within an arm's length before spreading its wings, letting out one last cackle, and flying off in the direction of the hospitals.

It wasn't a good omen. Nate remembered what an old fortune-teller told him at the county fair.

"Young man," she said. "You have a mission. The crows will let you know. There is something going on that others know nothing about. Be alert and receptive to your surroundings. But be cautious. Your life could depend on it."

Nate walked up to the end of the driveway and peered down the road. Call it a sixth sense, intuition, or a plain hunch, but something wasn't right at that old hospital. He hadn't even seen the old place and it was creeping him out. He heard the rumbling of thunder and in the distance saw lightning.

"Great. Flipping fantastic," he murmured. He was in the middle of a horror movie on his first night at his new home. He retrieved the last piece of luggage from the truck and headed toward the kitchen door.

CHAPTER 3

Nate had a half hour to spare before Uncle Nick picked him up in front of the school. He celebrated his two-week anniversary in Woodson by registering at the high school and taking a tour. He strolled over to the field and watched the varsity football team practice. They weren't bad, but it was obvious their strength and confidence came from their quarterback. Nate got up to rendezvous with his uncle when he heard someone calling him from the field.

"Hey squirt. Go out for the pass."

He turned around to see the quarterback throw the football in his direction. He took off running and with minimal effort the ball landed in his arms.

"Not bad, runt. Not bad at all. Throw it back to me," yelled the jock.

Nate flung the ball back to him and the quarterback caught it with ease.

"Good throw, rookie. You have a strong arm. You must be new

here. Haven't seen you around."

"Yeah, I am. Just moved here. Live on German Hill Road with the Drakes."

"Okay. I know your house. Just down the street from the hospitals. Have you seen any spooks yet? People say the old hospital is haunted."

"Nah, haven't seen squat yet, but I'm keeping my eyes open."

"You do that, runt. By the way, I'm Dylan. Dylan Pickens."

Nate was about to introduce himself when the coach yelled for the player's return.

"Dylan, you're holding up progress. Let's get moving."

Dylan gave Nate a thumbs-up and took off running towards the field.

When Nate and his uncle arrived back at the farm, the kitchen was fragrant with supper cooking in the crock pot. Aunt Nora set the table and Uncle Nick called first dibs on the sports section of the newspaper. Nate grabbed the comics. Although he still thought of his parents and brother constantly and knew the pain would never go away, he really enjoyed his aunt and uncle's company. Their conversations were interesting and you couldn't beat Uncle Nick's quick wit and humor. They were cooler than most adults their age.

After supper, they all pitched in to clear the dishes and then retreated to the back porch to finish reading the newspaper and enjoy a beautiful July evening. Max the collie was chewing a rawhide bone on the grass and Izzie's new foal, whom Nate had named Billy the Kid after the famous gunslinger, was relaxing on Nate's lap. Izzie, who had quickly recovered from given birth, was rolling in the dirt throwing her tennis ball in the air. Izzie thought she was a dog and mimicked canine behavior. She begged at the table, followed commands, and performed tricks, especially when there was a treat involved.

Suddenly Izzie alerted to something in the grass. Dropping her tennis ball on the driveway, she went to investigate. She sniffed, then pounced on the object. She grabbed the garter snake by the head and proudly carried it toward the back porch.

"Oh, no, you don't. Get that thing away from the house," yelled Nora as she flew toward the screen door.

Nate and Uncle Nick laughed, amused at the goat's conquest.

"Nicky, I'm glad you find this funny. That thing can keep *you* company on those cold winter nights," Nora said, trying vainly to corner the goat.

"Okay, Nora. I got your point. I'll take care of it," he said, retrieving a broom from the corner of the porch. He approached Izzie and knocked the snake from her mouth. It slithered into a hole, chased by an upset goat.

"Thank you, dear. Don't know what I would do without you."

"Any time." He winked at her.

"Oh, Nicky, I forgot to tell you. Folks in town told me that the new hospital is starting a work release program for some of the patients. They asked me to see if you'd be interested in employing one of them."

"You've gotta be kidding."

Aunt Nora shook her head. "Actually, I wasn't."

"I don't want any whack-a-do working for me. Got enough to do without having to babysit some looney-toon."

"Nicky, you could use the help. It won't be long before Nate will be in school. It's too much for one person, especially since you've planted the additional two fields."

"I'll manage. Let them find someone else. I don't want any crazies running around the farm, especially with you and the boy here. Isn't it enough we have the prison work details everywhere? Every time I go into town they're down there fixing something."

"You're right. But this is different. These patients need contact with other human beings -- to help them in their recovery. Won't you at least consider the idea?"

"No. I want no part of that social experiment!"

"Nicky, the ones chosen for this hospital program are like the Marines. They're the best of the best. I hope you'll think about it and reconsider. You'd be helping the community and giving work to someone who needs it. Someone who's stuck inside a building the whole day."

"Absolutely not. Conversation over," he replied flatly.

"Fine. Just thought I'd ask." She opened the front section of the Pittsburgh newspaper and started reading. "More missing cadavers from the coroner's office. Where are they disappearing to? They can't be getting up and walking away."

"Do the police have any clues?" Nate asked.

"No. According to this article the police are baffled. They have no leads, witnesses, or evidence. They're asking the public for their help, especially if they've seen anything unusual at night in downtown Pittsburgh. It does seem strange. You'd think somebody would have seen something."

"That's city folks for you. Too busy to notice squat. Wouldn't see anything even if it came up to them and bit'em on their rumps," remarked Uncle Nick, again immersed in the sports section.

"Nicky, just because you don't like the city doesn't make people who do bad. Not everyone likes country life. It's just a preference," Aunt Nora said, focusing her attention back on the article. "Anyway, people don't go out of their way looking for dead bodies."

"How do you miss someone dragging corpses out of a morgue?"

17

Nate asked.

"They probably drove a hearse and wore uniforms," Aunt Nora suggested. "They dressed the part so they wouldn't draw suspicion to themselves."

"Babe, you're probably right," Uncle Nick said. He turned to Nate. "I remember reading an article, oh, six months ago. Family had a closed casket funeral for a relative. The kid was ejected from his motorcycle. He hit the ground at 75 miles per hour. Killed on impact. There were pieces of his body everywhere. A little over here, a little over there --"

"Nicky, please don't tell this story again," Aunt Nora pleaded. "I don't want to lose my dinner."

"Sure, dumpling. But I haven't gotten to the point. The family had a closed casket. One of the relatives wanted to sneak a peek at the kid's remains. Guess what? There wasn't a body in the coffin! The funeral home was clueless, didn't have an explanation. Couldn't tell the family what happened to their loved one. They swore they put the kid in the casket. It was like he vaporized. The family sued. Mental stress and anguish. I'm sure it happened around the Pittsburgh area."

"I would be devastated if that happened to you," Nora said dryly. "After all, Nicky, I have big plans for you if you go before me."

Nick looked over the top of the paper. "Oh, yeah?"

"Definitely. I'm going to stuff you and prop you up in the cornfield, to use you as a scarecrow. That should keep those varmints away from the crops."

"Are you now? Well, I'm going to cremate you and use your remains in the kitty litter box," he said in retaliation.

"We don't have a cat."

"I'll get one," Nick said as they broke out in laughter. The conversation was a little morbid for Nate -- after all, he'd lost his parents and brother a month before -- but he recognized the affection behind the jibes and laughed too.

Nate worked off his meal by chasing the pets around the property. Tired by the heat and excitement, Izzie, Max, and little Billy found refuge under the lone oak in the yard. The animals rested in the shade as Nate contemplated climbing the gigantic oak. He grabbed a limb, hoisted himself up, and disappeared in the branches. Halfway to the top, he eyed a piece of paper tangled in a clump of twigs. He headed toward it, snatched it, and stuffed it into his pants pocket. Nate continued his climbing expedition until fatigue got the best of him and he descended.

Nestled between his animals, he retrieved the mystery paper from his pocket and read the contents. They were directions from John F. Kennedy International Airport in New York to Stonewood Sanitarium.

"Strange," whispered Nate. "Why would anyone want directions to a closed sanitarium in the middle of nowhere?"

He read on. The note included Superintendent Nelson's name and telephone number. Under this information was the following message: Boys - 7 and girls - 3. He was stumped. None of it made sense. His interest in the old hospital resurfaced.

The day was winding down and Nate rejoined his aunt and uncle. He kept the note a secret but asked some questions. "Aunt Nora, when did the old hospital close?"

"I think in 1950. There was a big scandal at the facility. After the investigation was completed, the hospital's reputation was permanently tarnished. No one would work there, let alone send their relatives there. Those poor patients." Nora shook her head back and forth.

19

"What did they do to them?" Nate asked.

"Son, some things are better left unsaid," Uncle Nick said. "Stay as far away from the place as you can. There are a million things around there waiting to hurt if not kill you. Why the interest?"

"Oh, just being nosy. No particular reason."

That much was true. Nate didn't have a particular reason for his interest in the old hospital. But something about it was calling his name, and he knew it would just be a matter of time before he paid it a visit.

Nate started reading the sports section of the newspaper when Uncle Nick made an announcement.

"Hey, guys. I know where those missing bodies are!"

"You do?" asked Nate as he put the paper down and stared at his uncle.

"Yes, I do," chuckled Uncle Nick as he lifted a hip off his chair and passed wind. "Oops, sorry. They're not in there!"

Everyone laughed. Uncle Nick was a real prankster. Nate excused himself from the table before the aroma hit.

CHAPTER 4

Nate rode his bike to the edge of the driveway. He stopped and looked both ways. A left turn would take him into town. Today, he was going right; the hospitals were supposed to be a mile down the road. He turned and stared back at his aunt and uncle's house. There was no indication anyone was watching. He made a right onto German Hill Road and started pedaling. Because the street wasn't a major thoroughfare he drove freely, straddling the white line and popping wheelies along the way.

The previous day, Nate had gone to the Morrisville Memorial Library in town and researched the old hospital. He discovered interesting yet gruesome information about the place. Located on forty acres and surrounded by thick woods and a twelve-foot wrought iron fence, Stonewood Sanitarium was built in 1850 as a state insane asylum. Its original function was to treat the mentally ill and reintegrate them back into society. A country setting was chosen for the hospital under the premise that fresh air would cure the patients. For a few years, Stonewood was a shining example of the best care money could buy.

However, by the close of the nineteenth century, Stonewood Sanitarium had become a prison, used to separate the mentally ill from society and any form of human contact. When patients arrived, they rarely left. Those fortunate enough to get out were usually in a wooden box. Contact with family members ceased once a patient entered the gates. There were no visits, letters, and with the invention of the telephone, no calls allowed.

To reinforce the sanitarium's "out of sight, out of mind" philosophy, the hospital became self-sufficient. Stonewood grew its own food, raised its own livestock, and repaired its own equipment. The hospital had its own barbershop and slaughterhouse. Patients were prohibited from leaving hospital grounds. Staff were the only ones allowed to go into town for supplies and equipment. The labor, which was tedious and physically demanding, was done by the patients and supervised by the staff. But even though the patients were used as "working mules," they weren't physically or mentally abused.

When Superintendent Schneider became director in 1940, however, Stonewood Sanitarium became a torture chamber of unimaginable proportions. An overpopulated facility gave him an abundance of human guinea pigs for his research. Volunteers didn't exist. Unwilling and resistant patients were beaten and many died at the hands of their caregivers. The dense woods surrounding the institution buffered the screams of tortured patients. Children weren't exempt from experiments. They were sometimes preferred over adults.

Dr. Schneider was an advocate of electro-shock therapy. He used it to treat virtually every disorder from depression, mania, and schizophrenia to truancy. Individuals were strapped to a gurney; conducting gel was rubbed on their temples, and electrodes applied. High currents of electricity were zapped through their cerebrums, sending the victim into convulsions and producing memory loss. Generally the memory loss, intended to interrupt the patient's disturbed pattern of thinking, was temporary. Occasionally, it was permanent. Such unfortunate patients spent the rest of their lives walking around in a robotic state, their memories, speech, and communication abilities erased.

Female patients were routinely sterilized to prevent them from bringing other "defectives" into the world. Residents became unwilling blood donors and excessive amounts were extracted from their bodies. Patients were dissected, dead or alive, to study their organs and anatomy. Patients were intentionally allowed to be bitten by poisonous snakes, spiders, and scorpions to test anti-venom drugs, some of which didn't work. They were immersed in cold and hot water to determine how long it would take them to die and whether they could be resuscitated. Known poisons were administered to patients in their food to determine lethal dosages and potential methods of treatment. Subjects were hanged, lethally injected, and electrocuted to determine optimal methods of capital punishment. The list went on and on.

Stonewood's "experiments" were leaked to the press and it became one of the biggest scandals in Pennsylvania history. The institution was forced to close its doors in 1950. Patients were transferred to other hospitals. Staff members were fired, prosecuted, and sent to jail for their participation. Until his death in prison, Dr. Schneider claimed his work was done for the "good of all mankind."

Although there was a significant amount of negative history attached to the old facility, there was the possibility some good could be found. The institution supposedly had an underground tunnel used by abolitionist "conductors" of the Underground Railroad. Hundreds of southern slaves were said to have used this tunnel as a safe haven, a resting stop, on their way to Canada and freedom.

Mulling over everything he'd learned, Nate rode by the new hospital. He caught himself, stopped, and backtracked to its entrance. He looked at the huge sign.

FOREST STATE HOSPITAL

Many years ago, Nate's research had disclosed, the state deleted the word "mental" from all the names of their psychiatric hospitals. Pennsylvania officials wanted these rehabilitation centers to seem like inviting, caring places where patients would want to come and families would feel comfortable taking them.

Nate peered down the hospital's driveway but couldn't see anything. There were no cars on the main road. He entered the gateway, remaining on his bike and pedaling slowly down the road. He listened for vehicles. It was so quiet he could have heard a pin drop. There were no birds chirping or leaves rustling -- just dead silence.

Then he heard it. Something was making its way up the road. It didn't sound like a car, but it was motorized. Frantic, Nate turned and looked back toward the exit. No, too far and not enough time. He dismounted his bike and steered it into the shrubbery. He flopped onto the ground next to it, peering through a small opening of cleared brush.

The rickety contraption was a golf cart. It puttered closer and Nate saw the vehicle's frame was nearly scraping the ground. The lopsided machine was so overloaded that the wheels looked ready to pop. The sign on the cart's side read HOSPITAL SECURITY.

"What a piece of crap," Nate said under his breath. Then he saw it -- or rather, him.

"Jeeezzzz," he whispered. "That's one ugly dude."

Nate couldn't take his eyes off the security guard. He didn't know if it was fright or fascination. This had to be the guy that Uncle Nick described. The guard *did* look like Lurch, that television butler. There was a little bit of Shrek mixed in with all that ugliness, minus the green skin, gap-toothed grin, and amusing personality. This guy probably didn't live in a swamp but he was more than likely born in one. He was twice the size of a professional football player and seemed rock solid. Nate was amazed the cart supported his weight at all.

He remained quiet until the cart passed. He decided to stay in his spot until the incredible bulk completed his security check. He didn't want to come face-to-face with this guy. A few minutes passed and he heard the cart make its way down the road. He peered out the hole. The cart was twenty feet past him when it stopped.

"Oh, crap," whispered Nate.

The big gorilla exited the vehicle, looking to his left and right. Nate's jaw dropped. The ogre was at least seven feet tall. His face could stop traffic, if not cause a few accidents. Above his rectangular jaw, a wide nose spread across his swarthy face. His eyes were embedded between an overhanging brow and sunken cheeks, and his hair didn't look like it had ever met shampoo. A long scar ran down the right side of his face. Yup, he was a mixture of Lurch and Shrek, all rolled into one.

Nate held his breath. His heart was going to explode. After what seemed like an eternity, the creature got into his cart and drove away. Nate wiped the sweat from his brow. He lay there until he regained his composure.

"Jeez, that was a close encounter of the ugly kind. What do they feed people up here?" he muttered, emerging from the woods.

He picked up a rock and exited his hiding spot. The remainder of his excursion would be done on foot. Marking his bike's location with the stone, he started down the road. He saw a clearing up ahead and ducked back into the safety of the woods, peeking out from the bushes to determine his position.

"Man, what a drag," he thought.

He was staring at the new hospital. It was an ordinary, mundane, reddish brick building. Manicured gardens and lawns surrounded it. Built in 1970, it resembled -- a hospital. It had a circular driveway spanning a huge visiting area, with patients and family members sitting at picnic tables and chairs. Nate shook his head in disappointment. He had been expecting something ominous and sinister-looking, something like a haunted house.

He noticed that the driveway split off, forming a road that went down the left side of the building. It passed a gate and guard shack. His eyes followed the wrought iron fence from its attachment to the right side of the new building to its continuance into the woods. Staying well within the cover of the trees, he made his way closer to the fence.

"Woo!" he whispered. "Now, this is what I'm talking about!"

Directly in front of him stood a dilapidated, two-story building constructed of massive gray stones. The few unbroken windows were boarded up with sheets of decaying plywood, some of which had fallen to the ground. Gutters and shutters were dangling and banging against the building. Birds fluttered in and out of holes in the roof and windows. Shingles, rubbish, and all sorts of debris were strewn in front of the entranceway. Moss covered the shadowy portion of the building and overgrown weeds, shrubs, and tree limbs choked the lawn and sidewalks. Stone gargoyles sat atop the roof as if guarding the building. Nate was in awe.

Then it happened. Someone or something touched his left shoulder. He was afraid to turn around, afraid to see what it was. Then he heard it speak.

"Boy, what are you doing?"

He slowly turned around and faced two gigantic legs dressed in black pants. He followed them upwards and gazed into the ogre's eyes. Nate heard a bloodcurdling scream and realized it was coming from his own throat. He started to run, hurdling anything in his path. He sprinted up the middle of the road, not caring who saw him, retrieved his bike and pedaled madly toward the exit.

Halfway home, he looked back but saw no pursuer. It didn't matter.

"Faster, faster," commanded his brain. "Gotta get out of here, gotta get away."

He made it to his house in record time. Nate thought his lungs were going to explode. He jumped off his bike, letting it fall by the barn door. He collapsed beside it, unable to move. After a few minutes, he got up and leaned against the massive barn, still unable to catch his breath. His head was swimming, so he closed his eyes, bent over and placed his hands on his knees while he concentrated on his breathing. The technique worked and within seconds he stopped hyperventilating. When he opened his eyes, a crow was watching him from a nearby fencepost. It cawed and took flight.

"Great. Just what I need," Nate said out loud. "I don't need a reminder. I got you the first time!"

He picked up his bike and parked it inside the barn.

CHAPTER 5

"Son, is everything okay? You're quieter than usual," Uncle Nick asked at dinner that evening.

"Oh, I'm all right. Just thinking."

"Anything you want to share?"

"No. I'm okay. Really I am."

"I know starting a new school can be hard. Don't be afraid. You'll fit in perfectly and be making friends in no time. If you ever want to talk, the door is always open. You know that, don't you?"

"I do. Thanks."

Nate looked up from his plate and smiled at his uncle. School was the least of his worries. He'd received the scare of his life and couldn't tell anyone, especially his aunt and uncle. They'd told him, on several occasions, to stay away from the hospitals. He'd disobeyed and betrayed their trust. They'd be disappointed in him when the gigantic creature knocked on their door and revealed his secret. In silence, he waited for the inevitable.

Although the incident scared him, he knew he'd return. He couldn't explain it, but he just couldn't help himself. He was drawn to the place like a moth to a flame. Some hidden force was luring him to the sanitarium. Something wasn't right at the old place and he had to find out what that was.

Everyone was comfortable in their spots in the living room. His aunt was knitting in her fireside chair and his uncle was watching television in his recliner. Nate was positioned in the middle of the sofa. Izzie was curled up on his left and Billy on his right. Billy's head was nudging him for a scratch. Nate smiled as he complied with the little goat's request. A sketchpad nestled in Nate's lap was rapidly filling up with detailed drawings of each hospital, and they actually weren't turning out badly. Yet something was missing. He couldn't pinpoint it but something was overlooked, accidentally left out. He looked up from his drawings to give his brain a rest.

The television was reporting one of the newest crazes in this country -- wild game hunting in the United States. Exotic animals were being smuggled into the country or stolen from zoos or airport hangars. People were paying big money to poach them on makeshift reservations set up across the United States. The popularity of the sport guaranteed no shortage of customers. Lions were the hunters' favorite, but it was a buyer's market. Individuals could order a specific animal and their request would be filled. It was a lucrative enterprise and authorities were having a difficult time identifying and prosecuting the guilty parties.

"What some people will do to get a head mounted above their fireplace," growled Uncle Nick.

Aunt Nora lifted her eyes from her knitting. Nate followed them to the fireplace where a twelve-point buck's head was proudly displayed.

"Woman, I know what you're going to say," Nick continued. "But we lived a whole year off of that one. That's the difference between country and city folks. We hunt to eat and survive. They hunt for...they hunt for... Oh, crap. I don't know why they hunt. Probably to fit in with the rest of the snotnoses."

Aunt Nora smiled, said nothing, and returned to her knitting. Nate turned back to the television program. It was ending, and the credits rolled over a screen shot of a dirt road leading away from the game preserve. He frowned, and a lightbulb went off in his head. He placed the diagrams beside each other and saw what he'd been missing. There was no road linking the new hospital to the old. Somewhere on the other side of the fence line, there had to be a driveway leading to the old building, and an entrance off the main road to the sanitarium. Tomorrow's plans would include finding that entranceway.

There was a knock on the door.

"Oh, crap. This is it. I'm done for," thought Nate.

Aunt Nora answered it. It was Jacob, their next-door neighbor.

"Howdy, Jake. What can we do for you?" Nick asked as he got up from his recliner.

"Evening, everyone. Just wanted to let you folks know there's a big town meeting scheduled for Saturday night. It concerns that new work release program the hospital is trying to start. Got some of the town folks all upset. People from the hospital are going to be there to answer questions and address concerns."

"I had a feeling their little project wasn't going to be popular," remarked Nick.

"You can say that again. Trying to put more screwballs out in public than we already have," scoffed Jacob.

"Listen, you two Neanderthals," Nora interrupted. "There's

nothing wrong with trying to make someone feel useful -- making someone feel they're contributing to society instead of being shunned by it. I think it's a wonderful idea and I'm all for it. You knuckleheads think what you want. I'm going to that meeting on Saturday and throw my support in for the project."

Nick rolled his eyes. "See what I've got to put up with, Jacob? This gal is opinionated about everything. Can't get a word in edgewise when she's on one of her rolls. I should have married someone quieter."

"Women don't come quiet," Jake said, and everyone laughed. "Big storm tomorrow, by the way. I'd start tying things down and storing things in the barn. They say it's going to be a humdinger."

"Will do. Nate and I will start taking care of it first thing in the morning. Thanks for dropping by and telling us about the meeting. I imagine town hall will be packed."

"You can count on it. See you there. I'll save you some seats."

"Thanks," Nick said as they shook hands at the door.

Before Nick locked the front door for the night, Nate summoned Max, Izzie, and Billy for their evening walk. The pets chased after him as he jogged up the driveway and turned right onto the roadway. A half-mile down the road, he spied a disabled vehicle parked on the shoulder of the road. It looked like an ice cream truck. As he approached, he read FREDERICK'S FROZEN FOODS -- PITTSBURGH, PA stenciled on both sides of the vehicle. Below this heading it read: *Ice Cream, Pizza, Meats, and Vegetables – The Best of the City Delivered to You.* Nate looked inside the cab. It was empty but the keys were still in the ignition.

"Hello? Hello? Anyone here?" called Nate. He heard a noise behind him and quickly leashed Izzie before turning around. A man emerged from the woods and started climbing the embankment.

"Hey, kid. Whatcha doing?" the man asked.

"Nothing. Saw your truck. Thought I'd stop to see if you needed help. What were you doing in the woods?"

"Taking care of business, if you know what I mean."

"Yeah, I do," replied Nate, taking a closer look at the man. He was dressed in black and wearing sunglasses, even though it was nearly twilight. His hair was slicked back and he was chewing on a toothpick. He was definitely out of his element in Woodson.

"Truck broke down," the man continued. "Waiting for help."

"You left the keys in the ignition. What if someone stole it?" Nate asked.

"How are they going to steal it? It's kaput," chuckled the man.

"I guess you're right. Can I do anything for you? I just live down the road."

"I toldja. Got help coming. Thanks anyways."

"Where you going? Isn't it a little too late to be making deliveries? And why are you dressed in black? The temperature has gotta be at least eighty-five degrees."

"Say, slugger. What is this, twenty questions? Don't you got someplace you gotta be?"

"No. It's summer and there's no school. Got all the time in the world."

"Like I said, you ask too many questions. Why don't you scram? Go play in some traffic."

"Okay, okay. Before I go, can I buy an ice cream from you?"

"Don't have any."

Nate frowned. "For real! The side of the truck says you do."

"Yeah? Well, we're all out. I told you once and I'll tell you again, get lost. You're getting on my last nerve. It's time for you to vamoose."

"Yeah, yeah I'm going," Nate said as he looked for Max. He walked around the vehicle and saw the dog sniffing at one of the doors. As Nate reached him, Max started to bark. "What's up, boy? You smell something?"

"Hey, kid. Get that dog away from the truck. Health code violations and stuff. I think I hear your mother calling."

"Funny. That's real funny. I don't think that's likely," Nate said evenly. He leaned down and snapped a leash to Max's collar. "Come on, boy," he said as he pulled the dog back in the direction of his house.

When Nate was approximately three-hundred feet down the street, an unmarked tow truck passed him, stopping beside the broken-down vehicle.

"Wonder where the service station is," Nate said, looking down at Max. The dog was licking at a dark stain on his paw. "Max, did you hurt yourself?"

He knelt to check the front paws of his canine companion. There was definitely something sticky and red on Max's right paw, but no injuries. "Strange."

Nate killed five minutes in the neighbor's field until he saw the delivery truck hooked up to the rig. The two vehicles moved on down the road, in the opposite direction from town. Puzzled, Nate walked back to the location of the breakdown. There were red droppings on the shoulder of the road where the truck had been parked. He stuck his fingers in the substance, rubbed them together, and smelled it.

"Blood. *Fresh* blood. Wonder whose it was?" Nate thought.

He wiped his hands with a tissue and headed home. Almost nothing about the guy's story rang true. He didn't look or dress the part of a deliveryman. He looked like a crook and Nate didn't need to be a rocket scientist to figure that out. The tow truck was headed in the wrong direction. There weren't service stations or repair shops on this road, only the hospitals and other farms. That so-called deliveryman was a shady character up to no good.

The sun was setting as Nate turned into his driveway. He peered down the road. No sign of the tow truck -- but he hadn't expected there would be. He looked down at Izzie.

"That's one guy that needed a good Izzie butt-ram. Isn't that right, girl?"

She shook her head in agreement as he unleashed her. Nate watched as she went tearing toward the house, knowing a treat waited for her inside.

CHAPTER 6

Nate was up early the next day completing his chores in record time. He helped Uncle Nick prepare for the approaching storm by corralling the animals into the barn. Equipment unable to be dragged inside was tied down with rope. Erie news stations issued repeated warnings of the storm's severity. The wind was picking up and clouds gathered on the horizon. The smell of rain was thick in the air and rumbling could be heard in the distance.

"Young man, where do you think you're going?" Aunt Nora asked Nate.

"Just need to check on something. Be right back," he replied as he jumped on his bike.

"All right. Don't go too far. It's going to be a bad one."

"I'll be back in a flash -- honest, I will," hollered Nate as he sped up the driveway.

He slowed down after he passed the Forest State Hospital sign. Nate kept an eye on the fence line as he swerved from side to side on his bike. Then he saw it: the entrance to the old hospital. He came to a stop in front of the massive gate. The words "Stonewood Sanitarium" were engraved on its front, half the letters welded on the left side of the gate and the remainder on the right. Cobwebs hung from the weatherbeaten and rusted bars; Nate had to clear an area so he could peek inside. Tree limbs scattered the grounds and the privet hedges had grown into shapeless masses. The once-manicured lawn had become a dirt field.

"Cool," muttered a mesmerized Nate.

He continued his inspection and then it hit him. There was no debris on the driveway. His aunt and uncle had told him, and the library research confirmed, that the old hospital was shut down. It wasn't used. No one went in or out, except Superintendent Nelson on his foot walks. "So why did the driveway look like someone has cleared it?" thought Nate. "It should look messy like the rest of the grounds."

He tugged on the padlock which was attached to a chain. Locked.

"Whoa, wait a second," he said as he took a closer look at the lock in his hand. It was new, and so was the chain -- not worn or weatherbeaten like the rest of the gate.

"Hmm, that's weird. I suppose Nelson could've replaced them," Nate reasoned as he gave the chain a final tug. Nothing budged.

He hopped on his bike and continued down the road until he came to the end of the fence. It bordered a cornfield. He'd have to go "off road" to continue his research. It started to drizzle and he decided to head home, knowing his aunt was right about the storm's severity. He counted the "Private Property" and "No Trespassing" signs along the way. There was one posted every few feet, which Nate thought was odd. Someone sure didn't want anyone snooping around that place.

"Too many signs. Overkill," thought Nate as he sped home.

He coasted his bike into the barn and parked it. Uncle Nick came out of the house and together they closed the barn doors.

"The animals will be calmer with the doors shut. It'll lessen the sound of the storm," said Uncle Nick as they jogged to the back porch. They had just made it up the steps as the downpour started.

The rain came down in buckets. Aunt Nora removed a fresh batch of cookies from the oven and placed them on a wire rack to cool. Max and the goats circled her legs, begging for a sweet treat.

Uncle Nick looked at the animals and then at Nate.

"Son, can you believe this! We better get our cookies before these fleabags get at them." He grabbed a handful and headed into the living room.

"Let me get this last sheet into the oven and I'll bring you two some milk," Aunt Nora called after him.

Nate followed Uncle Nick's lead.

"Uncle Nick, can I ask you a question?"

"Sure, son. What's on your mind?"

"Do you have frozen food deliveries up here? You know. Trucks that make house calls to deliver frozen food to people?"

"Sure we do. It's part of living in the country. Folks can buy their groceries from them without having to go into surrounding towns to shop."

"Do you know the name of the company that services this region?" Nate asked.

"Yeah, I do. It's Berrick's Frozen Foods. I believe they're out of Erie. Why?"

"Oh, the other day I saw a Frederick's Frozen Foods truck. Out of Pittsburgh. Thought that was funny."

"Well, it is. Jeez, what were they doing way up here? Maybe

they're trying to cut in on Berrick's turf. Heck, drug dealers and gangs do it. Why not businesses? I suppose everything is fair game nowadays."

"You're right," Nate agreed. Deep down he knew his uncle was wrong.

It was evening and Nate sat on the back porch watching the rain. It hadn't stopped but its intensity had lessened. The weatherman advised that the worst had passed. The rain would continue into tomorrow morning, and sunny weather was on the horizon.

A siren cut through the peaceful sound of the rain, and Nick and Nora joined Nate on the porch.

"That's the warning alarm. A patient has wandered off hospital grounds. Son, keep your eyes open. I'm going to check on the animals."

Nate nodded.

"Give me a holler if you need anything," Nick said, turning toward his wife. "Honey, stay alert. All you have to do is yell and I'll come a-running."

"Nicky, we'll be fine. Tend to the animals," she said, scooting him off the porch.

To occupy his time, Nate sat down on the stoop and started wrestling with Izzie and Billy. They were stronger than they looked and gave him a run for his money. Suddenly Izzie stopped nipping at his leg and went on full alert, staring at the barn. She jumped off the stoop and fixated on something.

"What's the matter, girl? What do you see?" asked Nate as he looked at the building. He saw a shadow. Someone or something was hiding next to the barn.

"Hey, you. What are you doing over there?" Nate yelled. His aunt and uncle came running.

Nate pursued Izzie as she led the charge against the intruder. The stranger began running across the yard, followed by one angry goat.

"Mister -- STOP. You're gonna run into the -- too late."

The stranger hit the clothesline at full force. It caught him by his neck and flung him to the ground. Izzie pounced on him like a rabid dog, tearing at his clothing. Blue pajamas. Hospital issue.

"Izzie, get off of him," shouted Uncle Nick as he pulled the goat off the frightened boy.

Everyone stared at one another.

"Son, get up. Don't lay in that mud. You're not a pig," Nick said, extending his hand to the young man.

The boy took it and Nick hoisted him off the ground.

"Don't be afraid. We're not going to hurt you, as long as you don't hurt us. Understood?"

The stranger looked at Uncle Nick and nodded.

"Good. Come on. Let's get you into dry clothes. Nora, you think you can round up something nice and cool for us to drink? Ice tea would be great."

"You got it. Even have lemon and lime wedges."

"Doll, you're the best."

Everyone walked toward the back porch. Uncle Nick had his arm around the youth. He was explaining the Pittsburgh Steelers' football strategy to their guest. Aunt Nora and Nate walked behind them. She made the sign of the cross. Izzie walked beside Nate, proudly displaying the pocket she had ripped from the intruder's outfit.

Ten minutes later everyone was dry and sitting at the back porch table. Nick had notified the state police, who were on their way.

"Son, what's your name?" Uncle Nick asked.

"Norm," he mumbled, devouring the cookies Aunt Nora placed in front of him. "Good, so good."

39

"Slow down, son. There's plenty to go around. No need to choke on them."

"Yes, sir. But they're so good."

"So, Norm," said Nate. "How long you've been living at the hospital?"

"What?"

"How long have you been living at the hospital?"

Norm stopped eating just long enough for a puzzled look to cross his face. "Don't know. Long time. Norm doesn't know."

"Must be a pretty interesting place. I bet a lot goes on there?" Nate asked.

"Yup. They keep us busy. No free time. Classes and work. No free time. Hate nights."

"You hate nights?" Nate asked, intrigued. "Why do you hate nights?"

"Noises," Norm said seriously. "Outside. Ground roars."

"The ground does what?"

"Roars. Ground roars. Lights in my window. Look out. Nothing there. Zoo."

"Are you saying you hear animal sounds?" Nate asked.

Norm nodded vigorously. "Zoo. Scary."

"Norm. Have you seen any wild animals on the hospital grounds?"

"No animals. Noises. Ground roars," repeated Norm. He seized his hair with both hands and shook his head.

"Okay, Nate. Don't upset our guest. Let's have a nice visit," requested his aunt.

The state police pulled into their driveway, and the trooper exited his vehicle. The front passenger side door opened. A short, chubby, middle-aged man with glasses got out.

"There you are, Norm. We were worried about you," he said. Nick stood up and the bespectacled man extended his hand. "Hello, Nick. Sorry for the inconvenience."

"No inconvenience at all, Mr. Nelson," Nick said, shaking his hand. "We had a nice visit with Norm."

"One of my staff wasn't watching him as they should have been. I hope he wasn't a problem," Nelson said, flicking his gaze from Nick to Nora to Nate.

"No. He was fine. No trouble at all," said Uncle Nick.

"That's good," he said as he turned toward the police cruiser and spoke. "Ralph, can you put Norm in the car? Thank you."

The rear door opened and Nate's eyes lit up like a Christmas tree. The Lurch look-alike emerged from the vehicle, walked up to Norman, and placed his hand on his shoulder.

"Come on, Norman. Time to go home."

Norman nodded. "Okay, Ralph. Norm had cookies. They were good."

"I'm sure they were," replied Ralph, leading Norm to the vehicle.

"Norman was one of the individuals we were considering for our work release program," Nelson remarked. "I'm afraid he's ruined his chances, though. It's too bad. He's a great worker."

"Yeah, that *is* too bad," Nick said. "I might have been able to use him here on the farm. But let me introduce you to the newest member of our family. Nate, come over here. Let everyone get a good look at you."

Nate, embarrassed to be the center of attention, slowly walked over to his uncle. He gave an awkward little wave.

"So, if you ever see this young fella wandering around, you know where he belongs."

Everyone laughed except Ralph.

"This is it," thought Nate. "I'm busted."

"Nice to meet you, Nate," said Ralph as he extended his humongous hand for a shake.

"Huh," said a surprised Nate as they exchanged handshakes. "Same to you."

Nate remained standing in the drizzle until he no longer saw the police car's taillights which vanished into the mist. Why hadn't Ralph ratted him out? He had ample opportunity. Could've racked up some brownie points with his boss -- but he didn't.

He liked Ralph. He couldn't put his finger on it but there was something about the guy you could trust. He seemed genuine, sincere.

One of the goats nudged his leg.

He looked down at Izzie. She was sitting on her hind legs, presenting her trophy to him. He grabbed the blue patch of cloth from her mouth.

"Good job, girl. Good job," he said absently, still giving thought to what had just transpired.

CHAPTER 7

It was a hot and humid night. Nate couldn't sleep. He tossed and turned, reminiscing about the previous day's events. He didn't understand; couldn't make sense of Norman's remarks. He knew he could believe only so much of what Norman said, but it was difficult to convince himself that he shouldn't give credence to any of Norman's ramblings. He scratched his head and looked at the alarm clock. It read 2:00 A.M. He got out of bed and walked to his window.

"The ground roars," repeated Nate. That phrase haunted him.

A breeze was blowing and Nate made himself comfortable on his window seat. His house sat on a hill and from his window he could see for miles. He peered out, scanning the darkness for activity. There was none. He saw the glow of lights from the new hospital; other than those, it was pitch black outside. He leaned his head against the wall, listening to the chirping crickets and hooting night owls. They had become familiar and comforting sounds to him. His mind wandered as he sat in the room's darkness.

It was August now, and Aunt Nora was already talking about school shopping. He was fond of his aunt and uncle but didn't need them to help him buy clothes. He preferred a drop-off and pick-up at the Cranberry Mall -- or the Salvation Army, for all he cared. He wasn't that fashion-conscious. But he was happy that Uncle Nick and Aunt Nora were eating this parenthood thing right up. Even though nothing could make up for the loss of his real parents, he knew how blessed he was to have fallen right into a family who loved him so much.

Suddenly the outside world caught his attention again. A vehicle's lights passed the house, headed toward Forest State Hospital. The lights continued down the road and abruptly stopped. The vehicle negotiated a left turn into what Nate assumed was the hospital driveway.

"No, it can't be," he said aloud, getting up from his seat. The vehicle had turned into Stonewood Sanitarium. He rubbed his eyes to make sure he wasn't dreaming. He saw the flicker of the car's lights through the trees, and heard the faint, faint sound of its wheels on gravel. Was that a car door? He pressed his ear against the window screen in hopes of hearing something else -- anything would be good. Dead silence. No more sound; no more headlights. Nothing.

He crept downstairs and rummaged through Uncle Nick's hunting gear.

"C'mon. Where is it? Where's that thingamajig?"

He dug deeper into the pile.

"Gotcha. You can run but you can never hide."

He pulled the binoculars from their case and ran upstairs. Lifting them to his eyes, he focused on the spot where he had last seen the car. Zilch. He was determined to remain awake and catch a second glimpse of the vehicle. But the sandman got the best of him and Nate awoke when he heard the rooster and felt the heat of the sun against his face.

Nate carefully packed his knapsack with supplies. He liked to be prepared, especially for the unexpected. He rechecked his bag, making sure he hadn't forgotten anything. There was a flashlight, extra batteries, matches, a small tool set, an orange cloth, paper, pen, snacks, and water. It was all there. He was ready for his expedition.

His plan was to continue where he left off. The hospital's fence line was bordered by the cornfield. This was good. It gave him ample cover. He sped down the road, hiding his bike in a clearing between the stalks. He walked the fence line down to its end. Determining the best method of entry onto the property was through one of the animal holes underneath the fence, Nate picked the biggest hole, grabbed a stick, and began digging to make it larger. Perspiration trickled down his face but he was relentless. He threw the excess dirt off to the side and his opening slowly grew in size until it was big enough for him to slip his body through.

He was in. He got up from the ground and wiped himself off. Grabbing his backpack, he extracted a water bottle, took a swig, and pulled out the orange cloth. This he tore into long strips. He grabbed his compass to get his bearings. The hospital would be straight ahead. Continuing west would keep him running parallel with the road. He tied a piece of cloth to a nearby shrub and entered the woods.

The brightly-colored swatches made excellent markers. He stopped every few feet and attached another strip to a limb or bush. He moved slowly and cautiously, making mental notes of landmarks along the way.

Before long his legs were scratched, bleeding, and covered in bug bites. He could see the shrubbery thinning up ahead, and he was grateful to be getting out of the thick brush. Using a piece of the orange cloth, Nate gently soaked up the blood from a gash on his right leg. Even with his wounds, Nate felt invigorated; he was finally going to get answers to some of his questions. Preoccupied with his injuries, he didn't realize where he was until he looked up and surveyed his surroundings.

"Crapola." He was standing in the institution's graveyard.

Nate wasn't expecting this. Cemeteries made him nervous, dead people and all, and this was the one place he had hoped to avoid. His research indicated there was one on the property; it was just his luck to find it. He heard thunder and the sky slowly darkened.

"Jeez, not another one. Give me a break," he whispered as he pulled a pen and pad from his backpack.

Stonewood Sanitarium had buried unclaimed bodies at this site. Family members were notified upon death of a relative and were given two weeks to claim the body. If they didn't, the poor souls ended up here. Because of the stigma of having a mentally-ill family member in the nineteenth and early twentieth century, most of the deceased came to rest in this lonesome field.

All the bodies were given their own number which was never duplicated. Their numbers were engraved on a twelve by twenty-four inch stone slab which was set on top of the grave. Any personal information -- including names and dates of birth and death -- had supposedly been recorded in a ledger, which mysteriously disappeared during the big investigation.

Nate looked at the rows of neatly lined graves. It reminded him of Arlington National Cemetery in Virginia. He bent down and looked at a marker.

"Poor guy -- or girl. Horrible place to be buried." He wondered who was lying here and how this person met his fate.

He decided to count and record the numbers on the gravestones. He walked to the farthest row, moving right to left, writing down the information. When he reached the end he started the second row, moving left to right. He worked his way up to the front using this zig-zag pattern. He was done.

Nate's growling stomach told him it was time for a break. Leaning up against stone forty-eight, he retrieved a snack bar from his backpack. He heard a screeching bird above him and threw granola crumbs onto a nearby dirt pile. The large black bird dive-bombed toward the treat.

"You musta been watching me. You're a hungry little rascal," chuckled Nate. He threw the varmint another morsel of food. His amusement didn't last long.

"Holy crap!" Nate screamed, leaping to his feet and darting down a row of gravestones. He turned to see a gigantic bat finish the last morsel of the crumbs. The creature spread its huge membranous wings, bared its fangs, and shrieked.

"Glad you enjoyed it, you freaking bloodsucker. Whatcha doing out in the daylight anyway? Thought you guys only came out at night!" He picked up a rock and threw it at the bat. It flew away. Nate grabbed the collar of his shirt and turned it upwards. "Not getting this neck. At least not today. This whole place is a freak show!"

Lightning lit up the sky, and Nate decided to continue his quest another day. It looked like he was going to have to race the storm home. As he zipped his knapsack, he got the strangest feeling he was being watched. Scanning the cemetery grounds, his eyes caught a small mausoleum tucked away in the corner of the field. A white mist hovered in front of it.

"What the heck?"

The texture of the mist seemed different -- more three-dimensional -- than the ground fog rolling in and encircling the grave markers. He walked toward it. A strong gust of wind hit him and he lost his balance. The mist was gone when he focused back on the building. He walked around the structure. All clear.

"Oh, brother. Like I said, a freak show -- and I'm the ringleader."

Later, back at home, Nate curled up on the sofa and reviewed his retrieved data. There were eleven rows of graves. The last eight rows had twelve stones in each line. There were only five markers in line one, six in line two, and eight markers in line three. Nate thought this was odd. He thought they'd complete a row before starting another. He looked closer at his data.

"Wait a minute," he blurted out. "That can't be right. But I'm sure those are the numbers."

"Nate, what are you talking about? What numbers?" Aunt Nora asked.

Nate realized he was talking out loud. He needed a quick explanation.

"Oh, sorry, Aunt Nora. Thinking about building a shelf. Messed up on the measurements. That's all."

"Nicky can help you with that. Nicky -- Nicky! Wake up!"

"That's all right. Let him sleep. I'll catch him later."

"You sure, honey?"

"Yeah. It's okay."

Uncle Nick opened his eyes and then closed them. He grunted, repositioned his head, and returned to sleep. Aunt Nora picked up a pillow and threw it at him. It missed. "Get more cooperation from a grizzly bear," grumbled Nora as she adjusted her glasses and returned to her knitting.

Several of the grave markers had duplicated numbers. Others were out of sequence. It didn't make sense. The farthest eight rows were correct. All the inaccuracies were in the front three rows. The total number of graves in the cemetery was supposed to be one hundred and one, yet he'd counted fourteen additional stones. Some of the markers had numbers higher than one hundred and fifteen.

"Doesn't make sense. I know I wrote the numbers down right," he muttered. This was going to bug him, and Nate knew it would be another restless night.

Later, in his dreams, an unknown figure was chasing him across the hospital's lawn. Hands were coming up from the ground and trying to grab his legs. He maneuvered from side to side to avoid being caught. The assailant was gaining on him. The yard seemed endless. He was tired but his fear of being captured was greater than his exhaustion and he kept running.

Nate awoke drenched in sweat. The last thing he remembered from his nightmare was a small boy dressed in knickers and a cloth cap, asking for his help.

"Man, gotta ease up on the sweets before bed. That was one bad sugar rush," Nate mumbled as he rolled over and returned to sleep.

CHAPTER 8

Nate tore his pants leg when it accidentally snagged a portion of the fence. He was anxious to recheck his numbers and considered it a small price to pay to get some peace of mind. The sun was glistening and the ground was drying from the previous night's rainstorm. He entered the clearing, immediately scanning the sky. He didn't want a repeat performance from his flying gargantuan friend.

Starting in the back row, Nate worked his way up to the front. He took his time, making sure to correctly record the numbers. He compared the information. No mistakes. Three grave markers had numbers above one hundred and fifteen. Six stones had repeat numbers, something his research indicated shouldn't be. He tapped the pen against his cheek, trying to figure out the discrepancies. He couldn't.

Nate eyed a dirt road on the far side of the graveyard, and headed down the hill toward it. He came to a split in the road, marked by a dilapidated sign with two arrows, one pointing toward the exit and the other toward the sanitarium. He chose the latter.

The building's front facade more than made up for the injustice of its side view. The old place reminded him of an English castle: gloomy, rock-solid, and downright eerie.

"Awesome!" Nate murmured.

The front door was hidden by a massive stone enclosure. To Nate's left, he spied the fence separating the two hospitals. Using shrubs and trees as cover, he darted to the entranceway. He jumped the crumbling steps to save time and brushed himself off once he was hidden inside the portico. He tried the knob. It turned and he used all his weight to push open the heavy creaking door.

Once inside, he turned to look around and found himself in a large waiting area. He studied the room's layout. An information desk sat in the middle of the room. Directly behind it was a door marked "BASEMENT." Two sets of stairs leading to the second floor were located on opposite sides of the central desk. There were archways at the foot of each staircase. Signs indicated that offices had been located down these hallways. Dust blanketed the entire area. The air was stale, the room cold and damp. Nate shivered and warmed himself by rubbing his hands up and down his arms. He gazed up, marveling at the huge chandelier.

"Wow. Mom would have loved to have that hanging in our dining room." He mentally measured its diameter at five feet. "Would've needed a bigger dining room, though."

Nate decided to search the first floor before heading upstairs. There was enough light shining through the broken windows to tell him he didn't need his flashlight. He stepped over the animal skeletons, crumbled plaster, and dried feces that littered the floor and made it to the corridor on his right, skirting the broken furniture and trash in his path. Ceilings and walls in the hallways and offices were stained with water damage. Nate rummaged through the desks and file cabinets, finding nothing interesting.

He was finishing the search of his last room when he spotted a painting dangling from the wall. There was something behind it. He lifted the picture off the nail, revealing a wall safe. Locked. Nate flattened his ear against the door and turned the spindle of the combination lock. The tumbler failed to click. He tried again but was unsuccessful. He began to replace the painting on the wall when he observed writing on the back of its wooden frame. Looking closer, he realized it was a three number combination. He set the painting back down on the floor and dialed the numbers into the lock.

He pulled down on the handle and the door opened. Brushing the cobwebs aside, he pulled a black leather book from inside. It was the missing cemetery ledger. He carefully flipped the pages, absorbing as much information as he could.

"Um," Nate mused. "Interesting."

Instead of taking the ledger with him, Nate opted to place it back into the safe. He knew it would be protected inside the compartment. He locked the door, placing the painting back over the safe to hide his discovery.

Backtracking to the main lobby, he went behind the information desk and looked through its drawers. They were empty. He tried the door marked "BASEMENT" and found it locked as well. He crossed to the other office area and found it resembled the other side, so he returned to the waiting area to ponder his next move. Other signs hanging on the wall revealed that patient rooms and the treatment area were upstairs. He deliberated, gathered his nerve, and ascended the wooden staircase.

From the upstairs landing, Nate could see that patient rooms had been located down long corridors to his left and right. He fixated on the treatment area in front of him. He took a deep breath and opened the door. The interior was dark and cold, like the first floor. He shone his flashlight around the windowless room. It was a smaller version of the downstairs waiting area -- the same nondescript architecture, the same filth and broken furniture. A door behind the desk separated this waiting room from the actual procedure rooms. He walked around the waiting room, poking the debris with a stick and shining his flashlight over the walls. One wall in particular caught his attention.

"Je...sus," Nate said aloud as he moved closer. Scribbled in big bold letters was the plea "SAVE YOURSELF -- THIS IS HELL." The message sent chills up his spine and he looked around for any surprises, afraid he'd be jumped by an unknown assailant.

It was time for the main course -- the actual treatment area. He stepped through the half-opened door and gasped for breath. This odor was different from the rest of the hospital. He covered his nose and mouth with one of his hands. When that didn't work, he used his shirt. It was a pungent, purulent stench, by far the worst smell he'd ever breathed. Nate guessed if death had a smell, this was it.

There were six rooms on each side of the hallway. Padded cells were to his left, treatment rooms to his right. A plastic mattress lay on the ground in each of the windowless cells. Moldy brown foam stuffing littered the room.

He entered the last cell and kicked the bedding aside. He took a step backwards as a squeaking rat emerged from inside. It ran from the room, upset that someone was tampering with its home. Nate shone his flashlight around that room as well. "HELP ME" was written on the wall in a brownish paint. Nate edged closer, putting his flashlight inches from the words. The letters had been written with a finger, not a brush, and the paint looked a lot like blood.

"Can't be," Nate said to himself. "You'd have to be pretty desperate to write messages in your own blood." But he had a feeling that whoever lived or died here was pretty desperate.

He crossed over into the surgical rooms.

Each room was equipped with a metal gurney. Hanging from the gurneys' sides were mildewed leather straps, used to fasten patients down. Antiquated surgical tools and supplies littered the floor. In the corner of each room was a metal cage, large enough to hold a human, and between the cages and gurneys sat some kind of squat rusty machine. Nate played with their knobs and wires, guessing these were the electro-shock machines. The electrode gel was hard as he banged the tube against the table. The sound echoed through the empty rooms, and he hoped the walls were soundproof.

The patient rooms were divided among two wings, labeled A and B. A concrete wall built at the end of A-wing separated the old hospital from the new one. The wall was identical to the one on the first floor, except this one had drawings crayoned on them. Nate found small trucks and ragged dolls in the surrounding rooms. He guessed this was the pediatric section. He picked up and looked at one of the wooden vehicles. It was a fire engine. He picked up another. It was a turn-of-the-century milk truck. The craftsmanship was superb. Nate had never seen toys built with such detail.

"Poor little rugrat. Can't imagine what this must have been like for him."

Nate knew better but couldn't help himself. He opened his backpack and gently wrapped the toys with a piece of cloth. He cushioned them as he placed them in the bottom of his bag. He was securing the clasp when he looked up There it was again. The mist. He saw it for a split second, then it was gone. He stuck his head out before exiting the room. It was clear in both directions.

"Been a long day. My eyes are playing tricks on me," Nate muttered as he walked downstairs.

He was tired and hungry. Nate pulled a treat from his bag and sat on a crate behind the information desk. His watch read 4:00 P.M. He needed to get home.

Then he heard the voices. Faint, but definitely voices. He got up and walked around the lobby. Nothing. He returned to the crate, and there they were again – two separate voices, engaged in conversation.

"What the --" whispered Nate.

They seemed to be coming from a wall grate. He knelt down beside it and listened carefully. Nothing, nada. He had just started to get up when he heard them again.

"Shipments are coming next Friday night. Everything ready?" the first voice asked.

"Yeah, boss. Things are good on this end," the second voice replied.

"Outstanding. This is going to be our best crop ever," replied the first voice.

"When it rains, it pours," remarked the second person. Nate tried to think. One of the voices was familiar, but he couldn't identify where he had heard it before.

"It sure does. That reminds me. How do the new workers look?" the boss asked.

"Good. Two of them just made parole. They're anxious to get to work and make some money."

"Wonderful. As long as they keep their mouths shut and do as they're told --"

"They know how the game is played. They'll keep their traps shut."

"We'll see. We thought some of the others were going to be okay, and you saw what happened to them. If these guys start yapping about our little project they'll wind up just like their predecessors."

"Got you, boss."

"Good. Let's get out of here. I have to get ready for a meeting. Contact everyone. Let them know the shipments start rolling in around eleven next Friday night."

"You got it."

Nate got up when he no longer heard the conversation. This was Friday. He had a week to prepare for the delivery. The voices had to be coming from the cellar, but the door was locked, and he hadn't seen any other way to get down there. He peeked out one of the front windows just in time to see a blue four-door sedan heading in the direction of the gate. Figuring the coast was clear, he darted back to the place he'd left his bike and made his way back onto the main road.

"How am I going to get downstairs?" Nate pondered all the way home.

He turned into his driveway. Aunt Nora was filling the bird feeder on the front porch.

"Nathan, did you catch any fish?" she inquired.

"Fish? Um, no. Guess I'm a lousy fisherman," he replied, parking his bike at the foot of the porch. He leaned his fishing pole up against it.

"Not even a nibble?" she asked in surprise.

"Oh, I got small bites here and there," he responded.

"Don't worry, dear. There's always tomorrow."

"You're right," responded Nate, his mind still occupied with the mysterious hospital.

Uncle Nick rounded the corner with a piece of metal in his hand.

"Doll, can you hold off dinner for a half-hour or so?" he asked his wife.

"Sure. What's that in your hand?"

"Slim Jim. Pete locked his keys inside his truck. I'm taking the Bluemobile into town to give him a hand. This contraption will pop the lock from the outside."

"What did you say, Uncle Nick?" Nate asked.

"Gotta pop the lock from the outside to get inside. Wanna tag along and keep me company?"

"Sure," Nate said, hopping inside the truck.

"Problem solved. Why hadn't I thought of that?" Nate whispered to himself as they turned left toward town. On his next excursion to the old hospital he'd check the outside of the building for an entrance.

CHAPTER 9

Nate was glad to be home. It had been a busy few days. After attending the town meeting on Saturday, he was off the next day with Uncle Nick to Ohio. They attended a two-day seminar on organic agriculture. Nate's mind was preoccupied with the old sanitarium and he didn't absorb any information from the lectures or exhibits. He had to find a way into the cellar.

Nate couldn't believe he hadn't thought to check for an outside entrance. If a basement entrance couldn't be found inside the building, maybe there was one on the outside. The very first day he was home, he followed his orange markers back through the woods, devising a strategy as he walked.

He started his search in front of the hospital, working his way to the back. He rattled every door, shook all the windows, and investigated every crevice and crack. He came up empty-handed. It didn't make sense. The rest of the hospital was easily accessible. You could get in through open doors and windows. It seemed the cellar was deliberately sealed to prevent entrance to that part of the hospital. He returned to the front of the building.

He decided to repeat a search of the first floor. There were a handful of niches he hadn't explored during his first visit because they seemed insignificant. He'd start with these areas.

The employee dining room was located in the corridor on the right side of the information desk. Like the rest of the hospital, it reeked of mold and was coated in layers of dust. He carefully stepped over the toppled chairs and tables. Mildewed floor-length curtains hung from the rear wall behind what had apparently been the service area and lunch line. Broken ceramic plates, shards of glass, and bent silverware littered the floor.

"Come on," whispered Nate. "There's gotta be an entrance somewhere."

Suddenly he noticed something strange. Soft sunlight streamed through the dirt-streaked windows on the right side of the room, but no trace of light made its way through the curtains at the rear. Curious, Nate clambered over the debris in the service areas to find out why. A plate snapped beneath his foot, pitching him forward, and he clutched at the curtains for support.

It was the sound that first caught his attention. He looked up to see the metal curtain rod detach from the wall. He had nowhere to run. He threw his hands in the air to shield himself from the weight of the rod.

It was a direct hit. He fell to the ground, entangled in yellow material. He sat up cautiously, throwing the curtain off to one side, making sure he wasn't hurt. He was thankful his outstretched arms deflected the rod from anything less forgiving, like his head.

"Jeez, I'm gonna be hurting tomorrow," he said as he slowly got to his feet. Staring at the newly revealed hole in the wall, Nate exclaimed, "Hallelujah! Ask and you shall receive!"

The opening was approximately five feet tall by three feet wide, with a rope hanging off to the side. He stuck his head into the shaft, looking up and down. Total darkness. He shone his flashlight inside. He saw a ceiling, walls, and an object dangling down in the shaft.

"What the heck is *this*?" Nate muttered, then he knew. It was a dumbwaiter.

There was one in the kitchen of his old elementary school. It went up and down by moving a rope attached to a non-electrical pulley. It was used to deliver items between floors. Nate grabbed the thick rope, pulling it in a downward motion. The screeching of the pulley lasted a few seconds and then he saw the platform rising into view.

"Man, how great is this?"

He secured the platform's line to an interior hasp, wondering if the platform would hold his weight.

"Only one way to find out," he said, and gently lifted himself onto the device.

"So far, so good," he muttered as he grabbed the rope. "Still good," he continued, as he unhooked the rope from its hook.

He started his descent, tightly holding the rope and giving it a little leeway to help propel him down. The dumbwaiter stopped. He was in the basement. He got out and found himself hidden behind a stack of wooden crates in a long corridor. The wall sign identified this as the west side, and provided directions to the kitchen, supply rooms, and maintenance shops. He started his search in the kitchen.

This side of the basement proved completely unremarkable. All the equipment and machinery had been removed from these areas and he was left to explore boring empty spaces. He prayed the east side of the cellar wasn't as lame. He couldn't help feeling that he was missing something as he proceeded to the other side of the corridor.

The east end of the basement housed the laundry room, dock area, and the morgue. He finished snooping in the laundry room and came back into the hallway.

Suddenly he noticed something he should have realized all along; it ought to have been pitch-black in the sealed-off basement, and in fact, he hadn't used his flashlight at all. Looking upward, he saw that the inset fluorescent lights glowed softly and unobtrusively from the dropped ceiling panels.

"Why would an abandoned building have electricity -- and why only in the basement?" Nate cracked his knuckles and continued his journey. Something wasn't right and he was going to find out what it was.

At last he found himself in front of the door to the morgue. Goosebumps appeared on his arms.

"We're getting to the good stuff. Dead people. Stiffs. Corpses. Cold meat. Worm food." Nate fell silent. "Man, I've been watching too many horror movies," he whispered as he tried the door. Of course, it was locked.

He looked up. There was a glass window above the door. Nate estimated it was an eight-to-ten-foot climb. He had two options. He could scale the jagged rock wall or drag crates to the door and make a stepladder. The climb would've been impossible if he had a larger frame, but fortunately, he was fairly slim and agile. He grabbed the edges of the rocks and pulled himself up. Wiping the dust from the glass, he peered in. The morgue was clean as a whistle.

"Why shouldn't it be?" Nate shrugged his shoulders. "Nothing else is adding up!"

The room wasn't just clean -- it was sterilized clean. The surgical tables, cabinets, and floors sparkled and shone. Everything was meticulous and in its place.

"Wow, it looks like Mom was here," thought Nate, as he jumped back down to the ground.

He continued to the loading dock and found the same thing. It was also spotless. Next to the conveyor belt, two buttons caught his eye: one green and one red. He hit the green button and the machine kicked into gear. Anyone who didn't know the location of this place would assume it was an operational business, needing only employees and merchandise on its conveyor belt. Hitting the red button, he turned off the machine.

There were stretchers in the corner of the dock, and next to them, a set of stairs leading upward. He climbed the steps and found himself in an open second floor office area. There were tables, chairs, and a locked wall unit. He started to snoop and found a key ring hanging on a nail underneath the console table. Every key that looked like it would fit the lock was inserted, until he was down to the last one. The device popped open and Nate's eyes widened as he opened the doors.

"Unfreaking believable!"

He was staring at eight blank television screens. He flipped the "on" switch. Pictures appeared on the monitors. Two of them showed the hospital's front entrance gate, but from different angles. One of the cameras was positioned inside the property facing outward. The other was outside the gate pointing inward. Two screens showed the front and back of the warehouse located across the street from the loading dock. Another camera pointed to the outside of the loading dock and another at the morgue entrance. The last two screens showed a set of doors to an area Nate had not yet located.

Hearing voices, he turned off the last screen and closed the doors, not taking the time to lock them. He jumped into a nearby fifty-gallon garbage can by the table. He was just closing the lid when he saw one of the wall unit doors was slightly open. He felt for the key ring in his pocket. It wasn't there. He peeked outside and realized he had left it on the table.

"I'm a goner if they come up here," thought Nate. He listened and tried to take shallow breaths in his smelly environment.

"This is the biggest shipment we've ever had," said the first voice.

"Yeah. Where there's a demand there will always be a supply," replied the second.

"Yup. Got that right. Ever wonder what happens to them once they're sold?" the first voice asked the second.

"Nope. And you shouldn't either. It isn't any of our business. You'd do good to remember that."

"You're right, but still -- aren't you the least bit curious who buys them and what they're used for?"

"No, I'm not. I don't get paid to think. I get paid to do. I couldn't care less. Let the world's humanitarians worry, not me. I just want my paycheck," the second voice said, annoyed. "Two shipments arrive Friday night at around eleven o'clock. Most of them will be out of here by Monday night, Tuesday at the latest. The third shipment comes Saturday night. Everything in order down there?"

"Yeah. It's been cleaned and we have food for them."

"Good. We have new men starting Friday. I want you to show them the ropes. Teach them."

"Okay. I can do that," the first voice replied.

"Good, let's get out of here and report to the boss. This place gives me the creeps."

"You first. Age before beauty," said the first voice.

"Yeah, yeah," said the second. Nate heard the first man start laughing.

Nate was soaking wet when he emerged from the trash can, half from his confined environment and half from sheer terror.

"That was way too close for comfort. Need to be more careful," thought Nate as he locked the cabinet and returned the key ring to its nail.

Nate saw no signs of the hoodlums as he made his way down to the first floor dock area. He wanted to complete his search before returning home. A piece of plywood was lying on the floor on the opposite side of the room. He made his way over to the sheet and picked it up, finding it covered a neat round hole framed in brick. He threw a rock into the hole and heard a plunk as it hit water. A well -- and a deep one.

Nate started jogging to the dumbwaiter. It felt good to exercise his lungs after his trash can captivity. Then it happened. Something grabbed his foot and sent him crashing to the ground. He couldn't stop his tumble -- only use his arms to brace for the inevitable. He half-expected someone to grab him from behind and jerk him upward, but when no one did, he sat up, spitting the dirt from his mouth. How had he missed that? There was a trap door in the center of the corridor; his foot had gotten caught in its metal ring.

He pulled up on the ring and the door sprang open, revealing blackness down below. He looked at his watch. No time to investigate, but tomorrow was a brand new day. He closed the door. Two more days until liftoff, and he had a lot to do.

He climbed out of the dumbwaiter. Unfastening the curtain from its rod was more difficult than it looked. Nate used the decorative frame of the opening to drape the cloth across the hole. It proved sturdy enough to hold the weight of the material. He wanted to keep his discovered treasure a secret, just as he had the wall safe.

Heading to the front door, he was passing the information desk when he heard the voice. It was faint but he heard it. A child's cry.

There it was again.

"Trucks. Can I have my trucks? Please, mister. Can I have my trucks?"

He looked around. He saw nothing.

"It's bad enough my eyes are playing tricks on me. Now I gotta worry about my ears," mumbled Nate as he opened the front door. He turned around for one last time and looked up at the second floor landing. There was a mist hovering in front of the entrance to A-wing.

"Great. That's just great. If I believed in them, I'd say I was being stalked by a ghost. Can my luck get any worse?" He closed the door behind him, glad to be leaving the old hospital for the day.

Chapter 10

Nate's aversion to the old hospital didn't last long. The following morning he was back, his emotions in overdrive. He was frightened yet elated, hesitant yet eager. He immediately returned to the trap door in the corridor and found it concealed a sturdy set of steps. He crept down the stairs holding his flashlight in one hand, using the other to support himself against the wall. His adrenaline was pumping and Nate felt his heart would explode from sheer anticipation. The excitement was giving him a head rush. He reached the bottom of the stairs, moving his flashlight from side to side. He spotted a light switch and turned it on.

"Man, oh man," he gasped as he climbed back up the stairs to shut the trap door behind him.

It was a journey back into time. Medieval times, the age of knights, crossbows, castles, fire-breathing dragons, and ladies wearing those funny cone-shaped hats. He was standing in a dungeon, the kind he'd read about in books and seen in movies. Nate stood between two cells which ran the length of the room. He glanced inside each enclosure. They were empty.

A single light bulb, the dungeon's only concession to the modern age, illuminated the cool, damp chamber. Flies buzzed everywhere, and some lay dead on the dirt floor. The cells were locked and the only way in or out was the stairs. There was one air vent in the room and it was built into one of the cell's walls. Security cameras faced each cell door. Bullseye! He'd found the last two camera locations. There were new locks in the cell doors, but the rusted metal bars and doors looked original. Nate shivered for a split second. He remembered how innocent and guilty alike were once housed and tortured in places like this.

It wasn't long before he succumbed to the room's stench. The smell was worse than that of the second floor. He wasn't an expert on bodily fluids but he knew the odor of urine, feces, blood, and vomit. The quadruple cocktail made him nauseous and he gagged as he ran to the corner of a wall. He felt better after hurling up Aunt Nora's good breakfast.

Climbing the stairs to leave, Nate hesitated at the top. His intuition told him there was something down there he was missing. He knew, from the voices, that they were using this area for something. But that's not what it was. He decided to do another quick sweep of the room to satisfy himself and put his curiosity to rest.

Going back downstairs, he instinctively headed toward the same wall where he had vomited, the one place he hadn't explored. Carefully avoiding his breakfast, Nate placed his hands on the rocks, feeling for anything out of place. Nothing.

He turned to leave when his eye caught a small shiny object protruding from the ground. He knelt down and dug at the piece of metal, but the dirt was too hard. Retrieving a small screwdriver from his backpack, he resumed digging and eventually loosened the soil. He uncovered another metal ring, similar to that of the trap door. He cleared the soil from around the hoop and examined it. Standing up and bending his knees for leverage, he pulled upwards on the ring. It snapped out of his hands and rewound back into the ground. He stood there waiting for something, anything, to happen.

"Come on. Come on. Don't have all day."

He turned to leave when a portion of the wall started to move. Nate stepped back as dust flew and a door slowly opened. Seconds later it stopped. The hole wasn't huge but large enough for an average-size person to squeeze through. Nate turned on his flashlight and peeked through the hatch before cautiously stepping in.

"Holy smokes. It's déja vu," he said, doing a three-hundred-and-sixty-degree turn with his flashlight.

The room where he found himself was the room of his dream – its walls lined with wooden beds, a stone fire ring in the middle of them. Candle holders were riveted into the walls, and used torches lay against the wall next to a pile of firewood. Nate placed his hand over the charred remains in the pit. Cold.

He spotted and picked up a scrap of fabric on one of the beds. It looked like a small piece of an old quilt. He dropped it onto the bed, thinking it wouldn't fit in his already jammed backpack, but then stuffed it into his sock to examine more closely when he had more light. He didn't bother looking for light switches; he knew there were none. He ran a flashlight down one of the walls, observing a glimmer in the distance. He already knew it would be a tunnel.

Leaving the compartment, he returned to the dungeon and pulled up on the ring in the floor. The secret door shut. He reopened it, and double-checked to make sure the dungeon's upper trap door was shut. Satisfied, he kicked dirt on his vomit and lightly stepped on the earth to hide the entrance hoop to the secret compartment. He wanted to be sure it was well-hidden, but he also didn't want to have to repeat the hassle of a strenuous dig. He turned off the dungeon's light and reentered the mysterious room. Pulling up on its door ring, he let it shut securely behind him.

Nate started down the tunnel using the distant light as his guide. It didn't take him long to discover he was walking in a stream. To avoid soaking his sneakers, he jumped up onto a ledge a few inches higher than the water. He heard crunching sounds underneath his feet and directed his light downward, revealing a trail of crushed rodent skeletons in his path.

"Better dead than alive," he said, nudging them into the water.

He continued his journey when, without warning, something slapped his face. He stumbled backwards, hitting the side of the wall. Fists in the air, he braced for the attack. Seconds passed. He continued to wait -- and wait. He picked up his light from the stream and shone it upwards. His aggressor was an extended tree root, significantly longer than what he had seen in his dream. Several of the slimy objects dangled down the path. He stepped closer to get a better look.

"Hey, what's clinging to it?" Nate pointed his flashlight directly into the eyes of a snake busily shedding its skin. "Oh, crap. My young heart can't take all this!"

He slowly backed away, pointing his flashlight up, down, and all around the tunnel. There were hundreds of snakes. He didn't like those odds. He pointed his flashlight to the ground and quietly pressed on. He was in their territory and knew if anything happened, he'd be on the losing end.

The light grew larger and brighter with each step. His pace

quickened knowing that it led to an exit. He kicked something off the ledge and heard it land in the water. Once he gave the right of way to a snake swimming upstream, he knelt down for a closer look.

It was a musket. Nate knew they were used by early settlers before the invention of the rifle. He picked the firearm up by its butt and tried to cock the hammer. It wouldn't budge. Nate laid the weapon back on the ledge, realizing time and the underground conditions had ruined it.

He continued toward the exit, brushing branches and limbs off to one side to free up the passageway. "This is my lucky day," he exclaimed as he emerged.

Nate knew his exact location. He was on the cemetery roadway, less than five minutes from the old graveyard. This road was his primary traveling route and he knew where everything was from this vantage point. As he headed down the road toward the hospital, his eyes lit on the old warehouse and his curiosity was aroused again. He remembered there were cameras monitoring the front and rear of the building. Why?

He approached the front entranceway of the brick building and tugged on the door. It was locked. Wandering around the side, he soon learned the front and rear garage door were too.

"What's so important inside that it has to be locked and on camera? And where are those instincts of mine when I really need them?" wondered Nate. He observed open windows on top of the building, but there wasn't a safe way to climb the structure. Patience. He'd eventually get inside.

Nate was also curious about the above-ground direction of the underground passageway, and he backtracked on top of it to learn its route. Pricker bushes nicked his legs and he made a game out of jumping over ant mounds. His walk led him from the woods to the hospital's backyard, near the dock area. He stopped at the forest's edge, not wanting to leave the safety of it.

And then he saw it -- a concrete foundation, its opening half submerged above ground and covered with a mesh grate. It was less than ten feet from where he stood, neatly tucked away among the bushes and tall grass. Nate walked over and rattled the grate. Although locked, it had some leeway, and Nate was sure it wasn't as heavy as it looked.

"What to do? What to do?" he pondered.

He pulled the tool kit from his bag and began to unscrew the bolts from the grate's hinges.

"Doing stuff a little backwards but what the heck. End result is the same."

He lifted the grate and gently laid it off to the side. Shining his flashlight inside, he saw that the interior of the cavern led to some sort of opening twenty feet down. A metal ladder bolted to the side of the wall made accessibility to this hole relatively easy. Nate tentatively climbed in and descended. The ductwork was comfortable for his size and weight, and he inched his way down the metal tubing, curious where it led.

About thirty feet in, he came to a split; the duct continued straight but a portion veered off to his left. Nate marked the exit route by leaving a piece of orange cloth in the duct that lead to the exit.

"Pays to be safe especially after my last screw up. Don't want to get lost down here," Nate reasoned, turning left into the secondary route.

The ductwork swerved right and sloped downward. He'd climbed this pitch before and knew he could maneuver back up. He slid down the metal slide, protecting his flashlight from damage. Nate knew he was nearing something when he whiffed something unpleasant. The putrid smell strengthened as he edged down the tubing. He eyed a grill up ahead. It was built into the side of the wall and the unpleasant odor was emanating from it. "Phew. Smells like that dungeon," he murmured, pinching his nose closed.

He breathed through his mouth as he positioned himself next to the opening and beamed his light through the grill. Bingo! It was the dungeon. He continued down the duct, reaching a dead end. He turned himself around and crawled back to the split in the metal tubing.

Nate crawled through the main duct until he spotted a faint light from another opening. This grill gave him full view of the loading dock. A second grill, located further down, gave him a bird's eye view of the morgue.

"Sweet. Real sweet. This is what I'm talking about."

He decided he'd investigated enough for one day and headed back to the exit. He placed the mesh grate on top of the opening, debating whether or not to screw the hinges back onto its foundation. A person would have to look hard to notice the missing hardware, and the loosened hinges would save him valuable time on later trips. He chose convenience and placed the bolts off to the side. He took a final look at the dock before heading home.

Suddenly he stiffened. *Danger.*

The noise was faint but close enough that Nate felt uncomfortable taking a chance. He wasn't about to jinx his streak of good luck. He nestled into the bushes and waited for the object's appearance. At last he saw it: a sedan pulling into the dock's entrance. The man from the ice cream truck got out of the car. After reassuring himself that no one was there, the man unlocked a side door and disappeared into the building.

72

"That guy has a set on him to be making an appearance in broad daylight. Gotta be an important shipment," Nate said, deciding to wait for the man's return.

It had been a good day. Nate's suspicions were confirmed. Unusual, if not illegal, activity was occurring at the old hospital. The man from the ice cream truck was somehow involved. Nate pondered what the guy was doing inside. He was more determined than ever to unravel the mystery.

Suddenly he heard movement at the loading dock, and the truck driver emerged from the building and drove off in his sedan. Raindrops fell on Nate's arms. A storm was moving in.

Nate had one more thing to do before going home and devising a plan. He walked back to the farthest row of gravestones in the cemetery. He stood looking down at stone ten. His research indicated there were several juvenile victims buried in this yard. One matched that of a little boy, Owen Medcalf, who died of pneumonia. In a private ceremony between himself and Owen, Nate returned the vehicles he had stolen. He buried the toys with their rightful owner. Nate apologized to Owen for taking them. As he left, Nate could have sworn he heard delighted laughter and a "thank you" from the gravesite.

It started raining and Nate jogged down the path. It was time to go home and devise a plan. Tomorrow was going to be a long day.

CHAPTER 1 1

Nate spent the day pretending to be sick. Another storm blew in and the combination of dark skies, cool breezes, and raindrops pattering on the roof made for ideal snooze weather. He awoke refreshed and ready to tackle tonight's mission. His alarm read 5:00 P.M.

Max was sleeping on the carpet, his paws on Nate's slippers. Billy the Kid was stretched out and snoring across his master's legs. Nate gently nudged the little goat to awaken him before getting up to look out the window. The rain had stopped and he shivered at the drop in temperature. His window thermometer read 67 degrees.

"Good night to be crawling around in tubing. Won't be sweating like a pig," he thought as he moved Max's bone from the desk to the floor. Retrieving the quilt scrap from his desk drawer, Nate carefully spread it out on the bed.

The fabric was old and dark, but the stitching -- what remained of it -- was remarkably sturdy. The design was a geometric eight-pointed star, its points spanning outwards from a central square. Unlike the thick fiberfill comforters he was used to, this cotton quilt top was backed with a thin piece of beige flannel. It certainly couldn't have kept its owner very warm; did it have another significance?

When time permitted, Nate planned to use the Internet to help him solve this puzzle. Hearing Uncle Nick calling him for dinner, though, he gently folded the quilt scrap and hid it in the back of his desk drawer.

Aunt Nora had prepared one of his favorite meals. Macaroni and cheese was bubbling in the oven and she was cutting hot dogs to mix in with it. It was a meal fit for a king. He gobbled down the last bite and wiped his mouth clean with the napkin before carrying the dish to the sink.

"Nathan, you seem a bit better this evening," Aunt Nora commented.

"Yes, ma'am. I'll be as good as new by tomorrow," he replied.

"Well, make sure you get enough rest," she said. "That's what you need to beat that flu. I'll check on you later."

Nate nodded in agreement and scurried up the stairs to his bedroom. He hated fibbing to his aunt and uncle but couldn't figure out another way to get the additional sleep he needed for tonight's mission. Securely shutting his bedroom door, he restocked his backpack with additional equipment. He'd borrowed a set of kneepads and a penlight from Uncle Nick's toolbox. Hopefully, he would have them back before they'd be missed.

Aunt Nora knocked on his door promptly at nine-thirty.

"Don't stay up too long," she whispered as she kissed the top of his head.

Uncle Nick wandered in and messed up his hair. "Good night,

buddy. Sleep tight."

"You too," Nate replied.

At ten-fifteen, he opened his door to see if the coast was clear. The hallway was completely dark, and even the sliver of light he sometimes saw beneath Aunt Nora and Uncle Nick's door was gone. Nate crept down the stairs, closing the front door behind him. He double-checked to see if the spare key was in its hiding spot. It was, and he locked the front door entrance.

He was at the cement foundation by 10:50 P.M, concealed behind the hedges. He removed the binoculars from his backpack and peered through them.

The overhead doors to the loading dock were wide open. A handful of men were sitting on the platform laughing, smoking cigarettes, and drinking beer.

"Hmm," murmured Nate. "Showtime's already started, I see."

A few minutes elapsed, and then a tractor-trailer came rumbling down the road. It stopped, and a man with a clipboard ran from the dock to the idling vehicle. After speaking to the driver, he pointed to the warehouse. The driver nodded.

Nate turned his attention to this building. Its bay door was wide open, and the group of men walked from the dock over to its entrance. They were joined by others who emerged from inside the building. The rig backed up to the building, stopping ten or twelve feet from the overhead door. One of the goons opened the rig's trailer door, as two other associates dragged a portable conveyor belt to the rear of the rig, attaching it securely. From inside of the truck, the same men retrieved long metal poles with hooks attached to each end.

"What the heck?" murmured Nate.

The men with the poles took positions on each side of the

conveyor belt. A third man came out of the warehouse dressed in full dog-handler regalia, and climbed into the back of the rig.

Nate heard a motor start up. The pole-handlers raised their rods outside the rear of the truck, clearly waiting expectantly. Suddenly they lunged forward and snapped their hooks onto something coming out of the open door. Nate lowered his binoculars, rubbed his eyes, and readjusted the lenses. He couldn't identify the merchandise. It looked like some kind of metal framework that was quickly unloaded onto a wooden pallet and moved down the line.

"You gotta be kidding," Nate said as the object came into focus. "I don't believe it."

The first cage contained a lion. The next two cages held tigers. The handlers carefully guided the crates down to the end of the conveyor belt where they unsnapped their hooks. A forklift picked up the pallets and brought them inside the warehouse.

Once all the cages were unloaded, Nate tallied the species on a piece of paper. There were a total of fifteen wild animals in this shipment. There were three each of tigers, lions, and wild boars. There were two each of gorillas, rhinos, and cheetahs.

Nate was amazed at the racket the animals made coming down the belt. The cats snarled, lunged, and swiped at their captors. The gorillas jumped on the side of their cages, attempting to separate the bars. They leaped down screaming and beating their chests. The animals were much noisier than Nate had ever known them to be at the zoo.

Nate remembered the television program about wild game hunting in the U.S.A. This had to be part of that ring. Distracted by the blast of a truck horn, he focused on another incoming rig. The truck stopped at the top of the loading dock driveway and backed in, guided by hand signals given by the man with the clipboard. Most of the workers disappeared into the doorway, heading for the back of the truck.

Nate suddenly realized he knew how to get a much better view. Putting on his uncle's kneepads, he opened the grate and descended downward into the ductwork. He quietly and cautiously crept to a spot where he could peer out through a grill at the dock. The loading area was a hub of activity. The wall cabinet was open and the monitors turned on. A man was leaning back on his chair watching the screens. A neat row of stretchers were aligned at the foot of the conveyor belt.

Nate focused on the conveyor, and sure enough, it wasn't long before it started to move. Large black plastic bags with zippers down their middle traveled down the device. Two goons lifted them onto the stretchers once they reached the floor's edge. They were wheeled away by a third henchman.

"Body bags. Wow -- it can't be!" Nate crawled to the morgue's grill and looked out.

"Hey, don't throw them on the slabs like that, you morons," yelled the man with clipboard.

"Sorry, boss. This one's a porker," the slimmer man said.

"I don't care if they weigh a ton. Don't do it again or you'll be taking their place. Got it?"

"Yeah, boss. It won't happen again," the heavier guy replied.

"Okay, okay. Let's keep going. We got a full load tonight. Angelo, did you remember to lower the thermostat?"

"Yeah. It's done," he replied.

"Good. The doctor doesn't want to cut into spoiled meat. He was upset the last time."

"*Superb organs and tissues going to waste.* Isn't that how he put it?" the chubbier man asked.

"You got it. Bottom line, less profit for us," snapped the clipboard guy.

"Hey, Sam. When will the 'bling-bling' load be here?" Angelo asked.

"Tomorrow. Midnight. Keep moving, fellas. We have twelve compartments to fill."

"Hey, chief. One last question. When is Dr. Death coming?" the chubbier goon inquired.

"Tomorrow, around 11:00 P.M. After he's done, we'll be transporting the parts the usual way, courtesy of Frederick's Frozen Foods."

"Wouldn't want to buy any food from *that* truck!" Angelo commented.

He and his chubby accomplice snickered.

"Yeah, yeah, enough is enough," Sam said. "Quit goofing off. Let's get the job done. You're getting paid to sweat, so let's see you do it."

They quieted down and got back to work. Sam left the room.

"Angelo."

"Yo, Tony."

"You think Dr. Millney is playing with a full deck?"

"Heck no. He's certifiable if you ask me. Nuttier than my Aunt Donna's fruitcake. But enough of the small talk. You know these walls have ears. You don't want our conversation getting back to the big boss, do you?"

"No."

"Then do what Sam said. Work and no talk."

Tony nodded his head and helped Angelo complete their task.

The air duct was located directly above the cooler. Although Nate's visibility was obscured, he observed the gurneys being rolled in and heard the bodies being hoisted onto the roll-out metal tables. He stayed until all the cooler compartments were full. Sam entered the morgue and told his men to meet him in the dock area. The lights were turned off and the door locked.

Nate crawled back to the first grill. Everyone was assembled. Sam spoke.

"Remember, men, silence is golden. Don't get drunk and start yapping about our little project. If you're going to stay local, keep a low profile. Don't get into trouble. If you screw up, trust me -- the big guy will have no sympathy. I want everyone back here tomorrow, around 10:00 P.M. Now, get out of here. I'm tired of looking at your sorry butts."

The crew laughed, grabbed their drinks, and headed out the door. Sam stayed behind with two men.

"Joe, make sure you check the animal cages once every two hours. Turn up the air if they do too much panting. Be on your toes. You know how the boss likes to make surprise visits, especially since this is a triple project."

"Got it, Sam."

"One more thing. Make sure there is enough grub for our visitors when they get here tomorrow night."

"There is. I checked on the stuff myself."

"Great," Sam said. "I'm heading out. Your relief will be here at sunrise. Remember, be on the ball. There's no doubt in my mind that the boss will be here later -- probably when you least expect him. Don't disappoint me. I'd hate to lose either one of you."

"Don't worry. Everything will be fine," Joe assured him.

"Later, guys. Stay awake," said Sam, giving a high-five as he exited the door.

The two goons made themselves comfortable in front of the

television monitors and began a game of cards. Nate looked at his watch. It was 2:00 A.M. Time to go.

Nate's suspicions were confirmed. The broken-down frozen foods truck from the other day was part of the operation. Tonight's "crop" was way different from what he'd anticipated. It shot his drug-trafficking suspicions all to pieces. As he headed home, he wondered what the "bling-bling" load was all about. It had to be something big. He pondered the idea of getting help.

"Would anyone believe me?" Nate thought as he pulled into his driveway. "Probably not -- they'd blame everything on my overactive imagination. A bored kid on summer vacation. Adjustment issues, trauma, something like that. Nope, I can't do anything, not yet. Gotta keep my mouth zipped, at least until tomorrow. One more delivery to go and it sounds like the most important. Then it's free rein and every man for himself."

He parked his bike and climbed the stairs. Tomorrow was going to be awesome; he felt it in his bones.

CHAPTER 12

"If it ain't broke, don't fix it" was one of Uncle Nick's favorite expressions. Nate agreed and continued his sickness act the following day. Aunt Nora talked about taking him to the doctor but Nate assured her he'd be just fine by tomorrow. He slipped out the door at 10:30 P.M., certain his aunt and uncle were fast asleep. He rode his bike to the hospital with a vengeance.

He had just passed the entranceway of the new hospital when his peripheral vision caught headlights in the distance. He stopped and dragged his bike and himself down the embankment. Looking over the hill, he saw the vehicle pass his location. It stopped further up the roadway and someone exited the front passenger side. They walked to the entrance gate of the sanitarium. Nate heard the gate open and saw the vehicle's taillights disappear inside. The gate was then closed.

"The good doctor arrives," whispered Nate. He dragged his bike up the hill and proceeded onward, making sure to detour around the cameras.

There was no action on the dock when he peeked through the grill. The men were lounging around waiting for the midnight delivery. The doctor was nowhere in sight. Nate crawled to the morgue grill and peered out.

What remained of a human cadaver was divided between the two operating tables. A trio in surgical gear were dissecting and dismembering the body. Plastic aprons, knee-high rubber boots, and facial masks completed their ensemble. Blood and other bodily fluids were everywhere, splashed, spattered, and smeared over nearly every inch of the hackers' apparel. The three figures cautiously circled the table, making sure they didn't slip on the dropped tissues and juices.

"Oh, man!" murmured Nate under his breath. "These are some really sick pups. This is unfreaking believable!" His years in science club had given him a stomach strong enough to tolerate just about anything, but he wasn't expecting such a gruesome sight. He quickly recouped from the initial shock. Still, it was ghoulish seeing someone hack up a human body and tear it to shreds.

One of the individuals seemed to be issuing all the orders, and Nate quickly concluded this was the doctor. His surgical skills, demeanor, and knowledge of the human body clearly indicated his stature.

"Gentlemen. Do not hack at the bones. Saw them smoothly. That's how the companies like to receive them. Neat and tidy. They don't like jagged or rough edges. Arthur, help me remove this section of skin. We have nice patches over here."

"Doc, come on. Do I have to? I didn't realize that part of my job duties included chopping people up."

"Arthur, we are not chopping up anything. We are gently removing parts. There will always be muscles, tendons, and blood vessels that need an extra pull or two. Most will separate quite nicely."

"Doc, I'm going to puke. This isn't football. I don't need play-by-play coverage."

"Arthur, I'm sorry you feel that way. If you can't handle what we're doing, then maybe you need to leave. Send someone back that has a stronger stomach. We have quite a few more bodies to harvest."

"Just give me a minute, okay? I'll be all right. This just takes a little getting used to. How do you do it? I mean cutting up bodies," he asked the doctor.

"Arthur, I've been a doctor for over thirty years. When someone dies they're just a piece of meat -- no different than a cow or pig. Have you ever been to a slaughterhouse?"

"Yeah."

"Fascinating places to visit. Anyway, compare it to that. Let's continue. We're running behind with these needless interruptions."

"Doc, one more thing. How do you know the parts we're removing are in good shape? You know. Not diseased or rotten."

"It honestly doesn't matter, and it's none of your concern. A piece of advice. Keep your mouth shut and mind your business. Do your job and maybe you'll live long enough to spend the good money you're making. Understand?"

"Yeah. Message received."

The trio resumed working. Gruesome as the ordeal was, Nate found it fascinating. He was amazed how quickly a body could be dissected. It was like watching his dad carve the Thanksgiving turkey. The doctor made it look elegant, almost an art. Precision cuts around the bones, remove the meat, and then scoop out the stuffing -- only in this case the stuffing was human tissue and organs.

Sam, the second in command, entered the room. He surveyed the scene and turned around to face the door, patting his forehead with a handkerchief.

"Hey, doc. How's it going in here?" he asked.

"Splendid. We're almost done. Two more to do."

"Great. The boss just arrived. He'll be in to see you shortly."

"Wonderful. What's the matter, Samuel? Feeling squeamish?"

"I'm okay. Just not my cup of tea."

"I'm sorry to hear that, Samuel. You prefer murdering people to dismembering them?"

"If you put it that way, yes. I'll leave the slicing and dicing to you. You're the expert."

"I am. It's like I was born to do it. As you say, it's my cup of tea."

"Whatever," Sam said, pulling the door open to leave.

"Good-bye, Samuel. Enjoy your Labor Day holiday."

"Sure, you too," he said on his way out.

"Wimp," one of his co-workers yelled after him.

The doctor lifted up his head and laughed. Nate shivered. The shrill sound, almost a shriek, reminded him of the mad doctor in those Frankenstein movies. The doctor continued chuckling as his two assistants looked at each other, shrugged their shoulders, and continued working.

"Don't worry, fellas. I'm not crazy. Just had a funny thought," the doctor said, struggling to control his hysteria.

"Thought you were laughing at the wimp remark," Arthur said.

"No, I wasn't. Although it *was* funny. Comrades, let's roll in those empty caskets. While one of you helps me finish, the other can be disposing of the waste."

Nate watched in astonishment as the leftover body parts were packed unceremoniously into coffins. Twelve bodies equaled three full caskets. Arthur hosed off the tables and floor, directing the flow of fluids into a floor drain.

Then the door opened.

"Holy smokes," remarked Nate as he rubbed his eyes in astonishment. "I wouldn't have believed it if I hadn't seen it with my own two eyes!"

"Superintendent Nelson. It's nice of you to grace us with your presence. Would you like to join our little party?"

"It's always a pleasure to see you, Dr. Millney, but no, I wouldn't. How are things progressing?"

"Splendid. We're done. Just cleaning up. It makes it easier when they're young and lean. Cutting through extra fat makes it difficult and time-consuming."

"Wouldn't know about that. That's why I hired you."

"Yes. I know."

"Has the merchandise been packaged for delivery?" Nelson asked as he turned toward Arthur.

"The coolers and boxes are almost done. They'll be wheeled to the truck shortly," he replied.

"Good. What about the waste?"

"In the caskets. Gus and a few others will be taking them to the cemetery for burial."

"Make sure they have headstones. I don't want anything drawing suspicion to our operation."

"No problem."

"Dr. Millney, I'll be talking to you after the Labor Day holiday. I'm lining up another delivery as we speak. In the meantime, I hope you'll excuse me. I have to make sure the consent forms and death certificates look legitimate, so they can be mailed out to our associates later this evening."

"Good work, Nelson. You're a man who pays attention to detail. I admire that quality in a person."

"I have to be. One little screw-up could land us all in prison," the superintendent replied.

"Quite so," the doctor agreed. "I don't think people would appreciate us carving up their relatives."

"The families are not my concern. I don't think we'd get a warm prison reception if the inmates and staff found out why we were there." Nelson shuddered at the thought. "No, it's imperative we keep a low profile and not draw attention to this hospital. Things must be perfect."

"And they always are."

"Good," Nelson said. "I have to be going; my other shipment should be arriving shortly, and as I mentioned, I have things to do. Doc, thanks again. Be expecting that call soon. Superb work as usual."

"Thank you, sir. Au revoir," said Millney, with a slight ceremonial bow.

The trio resumed cleaning. The place was well on its way to spotless in a matter of minutes. The doctor said something to his two associates, shook hands, and left the room. The two finished tidying the morgue.

"So, Art. Who do you think is crazier? The doctor or Nelson?" Arthur's partner in crime asked.

"It's a close call. I think one's just as whacked as the other."

"Yeah. The wheels are spinning but the hamsters are dead."

Arthur laughed. "Their elevators don't go all the way to the top. Heck, they don't even make it off the ground floor!"

"Yeah. What's that phrase my nephew says? They have a full

sixpack -- they just lack the plastic thingy that holds it all together."

Art grinned and nodded his head.

"Art."

"What?"

"Do you think that a person knows they're insane? You know cuckoo?"

"Not those two, anyway. But who cares, as long as their money's good." Arthur scanned the area. "Well, things look okay in here. We'd better join the others. And this conversation, the one we just had, never occurred. Got it?"

"You bet. Mum's the word," said Art's associate, putting his finger to his lips.

"I mean it. Keep it zipped. Don't want it getting back to the big guy that we think he's a loon."

"I get it. You don't have to tell me twice."

"Good. Let's get going."

Nate felt the cramps subside as he leaned back to stretch his legs. It was hard to believe, but Superintendent Nelson really was the mastermind behind this entire operation. No one would suspect a man in his position to be the brains behind such a horrible thing. But only a man in his position would have the power to pull off a caper like this one. No one would question his motives -- and he had access to both hospitals. "Now, it's just a matter of stopping him," thought Nate.

He heard a truck backing into the loading dock. Round two was beginning.

CHAPTER 13

Nate used his knapsack to prop up his upper body. He needed to get comfortable, not knowing how long this exploit would last. He looked out of the grill and noticed a rig backed into the dock, but there was no activity. Nelson, Sam, and a handful of their cronies were talking on the corner of the platform.

Nate's mind wandered. He thought of his brother Eric, who would have loved being part of this. Despite their teasing, Eric had always been there for Nate, in good times and bad. Nate would have given anything to share this adventure with him.

His thoughts were interrupted by the singing of a black man who exited the restroom on the dock's landing. He approached the group, wiping his hands with a paper towel. Pretending it was a basketball, he shot it into a nearby trash can. He said something to the group that Nate did not hear, and everyone burst into laughter. Nate prayed they'd move closer so he could better eavesdrop on their conversation. Slowly but surely they inched his way.

"Thanks, big guy," the black man said as he headed toward the rear of the truck. "Traffic was backed up for miles on the New Jersey Turnpike. An accident. We lost time but we made up for it once we crossed the state line. It was smooth sailing the whole trip on Route 80. We made one pit stop along the way. You know, to accommodate our guests."

"Your usual spot? The Bellefonte exit?" Sam asked.

"Yeah. Everyone behaved this time. Didn't have to kill anyone." He and Sam started to laugh.

"Gangster humor," whispered Nate, hoping that was all it was.

"Okay, guys. You're not performing at a comedy club. Enough of the bull," Nelson barked. "What do you have for us this time?"

He crossed his arms, waiting.

"Boss, you're going to love this load. They're feistier, younger, healthier than the last bunch. We have some real lookers in this group. Rebels burned their village and killed everyone. Three girls and seven boys."

"Let's have a peek. Open the door," ordered Nelson.

Nate's brow furrowed. Rebels? Village? He didn't recall seeing anything on TV or in the papers about anything like that. He prepared for the unloading of the "bling-bling" cargo.

The truck's rear door opened and the merchandise was escorted down the ramp. They were Asian teens, about his age, their hands and feet bound by rope. They were barefoot, shabbily dressed, and dirty. Their captors yelled commands at them and they returned puzzled, blank stares. Nate guessed they didn't understand English. One of their captors cracked a whip and hit the side of the truck. The scared teens hobbled quickly down the ramp and lined up beside one another on the dock.

Superintendent Nelson approached the juveniles. He circled

them, examining them from head to toe. He stopped in front of each one, inspecting his or her face and overall physique. He seemed pleased with this shipment -- especially a girl of about thirteen, standing at the end of the line.

"This one is quite lovely, a delightful creature," he said, lifting her head by placing his finger underneath her jaw.

"Yes, she is," replied the black man.

"She's so innocent looking, so sweet. We'll get top dollar for her. Know anything about her, Marcel? Has she been broken in?" Nelson asked.

"Don't know. None of them speak or understand English. They speak that foreign mumbo jumbo. Some Chinese crap. Don't know what dialect it is. No information on that girl's virginity -- although I can find out for you if you want."

Marcel grinned, giving a lustful smile to the pretty girl at the end.

"Touch her and I'll have you hung upside down by your feet," remarked Nelson. "I'll cut out your tongue and slice you from neck to groin. I'll use your intestines as a jump rope. Oh, did I mention you'll be alive when all of this was going on?"

"Boss, it was a joke. Just a little humor," Marcel said, raising his hands and backing off.

Superintendent Nelson turned and faced his other employees.

"No one is to touch or lay a hand on any of our guests. The consequences will be deadly. Am I understood?"

The workers nodded their heads.

"Good. Gentlemen, make no mistake. This group is a money-maker, especially her," he said, pointing at the petite beauty. "Our buyers will pay a hefty price to own any one of them. I want our guests to remain bruise free -- along with other things," he added, turning to look at Marcel.

91

"Boss, I got your hint the first time. No problems on this end. We're good."

"Wonderful. Bring our guests to the dungeon. I have calls to make. Marcel, I'll see you upstairs by the console."

Nelson walked away, punching numbers into his cell phone, Marcel in tow.

Nate watched as one of the men walked over to the trap door. Opening it, the goon signaled the others to bring the captives his way.

The man with the whip cracked it at the youths. Intentional or not, the tip hit the pretty girl and she cried out in pain. She fell to the floor, nursing her injury. One of the captives, a boy dressed in brown, scurried to her aid. He knelt down beside her and curled his arm around her, comforting her in their native tongue. She nodded as he helped her up.

"Isn't that sweet. Boyfriend and girlfriend," remarked Whip Man. His associates chuckled.

The kid dressed in brown gave Whip Man the evil eye and spat out a few words in his native tongue. When Whip Man laughed, the kid lunged at him, knocking the gangster to the ground and delivering a fierce right hook to his jaw. The whip flew out of the man's hands. Whip Man was receiving the beating of his life.

"Good for you! Kick him in the ribs! Pound his face into the ground! Give him a left and another right! Give fat boy the butt-whipping he deserves," Nate cheered silently.

"Get him off me! Get him off me!" yelled Whip Man as the youth continued his assault.

The boy was restrained by his other captors. Bleeding from his nose and mouth, Whip Man got up from the ground. He wiped his nose with the back of his hand.

"You little piece of crap," he yelled. "Tie Judo Joe to that post.

He's got a lesson to learn."

Picking up his switch, Whip Man lifted it in the air and cracked it.

Nate couldn't tell the direction of the gunshot. But suddenly Whip Man fell to the ground, clutching his chest. Blood stained his shirt and the injured man gasped for breath. Superintendent Nelson approached him, a 9mm in his hand. The man Nelson called Marcel stood by his side.

"Hey, stupid. Didn't I tell you not to mess with the merchandise?" Nelson scanned his frightened workers and shook his head. "There's always one that doesn't like to play by the rules."

He pointed the weapon at Whip Man's head and pulled the trigger. The Asian teens screamed at the blast. The workers knew better.

"Gentlemen, consider this a learning experience," Nelson said. "I won't let anyone get in my way. I killed those reporters from Pittsburgh and I'll kill any one of you. Do not test me. I will say it one more time. Do not touch the wares."

He calmly opened his windbreaker and holstered his weapon. He then turned towards Sam. "Get rid of the body. Feed him to the animals. Give them a treat of fresh meat. Or, if you don't feel like making the trip, you can dump him in the well over there." Nelson pointed at the piece of plywood. "Doesn't much matter to me."

"Yes, boss," replied Sam, turning toward the thug on his right. "Tony, take the kids downstairs."

"Wait," Nelson interrupted. "Bring the feisty one to me."

Tony grabbed the rambunctious youth and stood him in front of Nelson. Nelson grabbed the youth's head, locking his face between his two hands, making sure the youth saw his face.

"Son. I know you don't understand a word I'm saying but I'm going to say it anyway. Pull a stunt like that again and you're dead.

This is your second chance. You don't get a third."

Nelson released his grip from the youth and pointed his finger at him. "Understand?"

The teen moved his head up and down.

"Good. Take him away and put him with the others," ordered Nelson as he straightened his jacket and glasses. He watched as Tony encircled the youths and guided them toward the stairs. "Sam, I'm waiting for some calls. I'll be upstairs by the console if you need me."

"Got it, boss. I'll give you a holler if we need anything."

"You do that." Nelson turned toward Marcel and together they went upstairs.

Nate scurried like a squirrel to the dungeon's grill. The boys and girls were separated. The boys had been thrown into the cell right below him. The girls were on the opposite side, embracing each other and crying. The rebellious teen in brown gathered the males in a huddle and began talking to them.

A light appeared between the cells and Nate knew someone had opened the trap door. Nelson, Sam, and two henchmen came downstairs. Their noses and mouths were covered by face masks.

"It's too bad we can't use the ventilation system. This place stinks," Sam complained.

"I know," Nelson replied. "But it's too noisy when it's on. I don't want anything drawing attention to our operation."

"Couldn't we set up a portable unit?" Sam asked.

"Sam, are you getting soft on me? You can't smell the stench when you're upstairs, can you? No one has to come down here unless it's necessary. That's why we have the cameras. *They* --" Nelson said, turning to look at his captives, " -- won't have to put up with it for much longer. I have buyers lined up ready to bid on them. They'll be gone by Monday night, Tuesday at the latest."

"Gotcha. Anything else?" Sam asked.

"Have all the keys been put on the one ring and triple sets made? I don't want lost keys like the last time."

"Done. I have one set. Here's yours. The other key ring is by the monitors."

"Excellent. Make sure the animals are checked every two hours. We're going to ship them the same night as the kids."

"Where are the animals and kids going to?" Sam asked.

"Sam, are you writing a book? None of your business. Let me worry about that. I hired you to supervise those numbskulls upstairs, not to play twenty questions."

"Sorry, boss. Nothing meant by it."

"Okay, okay. Forget about it. Let's get going with the pictures. Give each side a pan of water, towels, and some soap. Get them cleaned up. Then escort them, one at a time, upstairs. Gary is ready with the camera. The buyers are anxious to look at the wares."

"Got it, boss."

"After all of their snapshots have been taken, give them some food and water. I smell a tidy profit from this group. These are the best we've ever had."

"Cha-ching, cha-ching. Right, boss?" Sam grinned.

"Absolutely. I smell our bank accounts getting fatter. God bless slavery. It's alive and well in the twenty-first century. Who would've believed it? And Sam --"

"Yes, boss?"

"Be careful with that one." Nelson pointed to the youth dressed in brown clothes. "He might be a little too healthy for his own good."

"Will do. Will do."

Nate waited until the whole photo processing was done. He then crawled back to the dock vent for a last look. Two goons were watching the television monitors. The clock on the wall read 3:00 A.M. It was time to go home. He needed some sleep and time to develop a plan.

He closed the grill and walked just inside the woods bordering the dirt road. The graveyard was in sight. "Hey Nate. Over here."

He stopped dead in his tracks. He looked toward the woods but didn't see a thing. He did a three-sixty, peering down the road and wood line. Nothing. Then he heard the voice again.

"I want to help you. Over here," pleaded the voice. The bushes started rustling and he saw something or someone emerging from them.

Petrified, Nate ran straight up the middle of the road, leaving the safety and concealment of the woods. There was a grassy section straight ahead that would cut his traveling time by a few seconds. He headed toward it.

And there it was, out of nowhere. The mist. It hovered over the turf he was fast approaching. As Nate watched, an extended arm formed out of the mist, pointing him away from the grassy area. Without hesitation or thought, Nate veered back onto the roadway.

Too frightened to look back, he ran down the path, scrambled under the fence and jumped into the cornstalks. He waited for his pursuer but no one followed. After a few minutes he emerged from his hiding spot.

"Weird," muttered Nate as he grabbed his bike. "Why didn't he chase me? Who was that, anyhow? And what was with the mist?"

"Just what I need. Another mystery to solve," he thought as he sped away from the property on his bike.

CHAPTER 14

Nate, Uncle Nick, and Aunt Nora walked down the church steps after congratulating Father Hogan on a particularly stirring homily. Nick and Nora stopped at the foot of the steps to chat with neighbors, but Nate was more than ready to go home. When Aunt Nora commented on how fidgety Nate seemed during the entire Mass, he blamed it on new school jitters. In reality, though, he was wired up for tonight's mission. He still needed to work out a few kinks but overall his escape plan was solid. Professionals couldn't have done a better job. Nate was proud and ready to execute his game plan.

"Nicky, do you mind if I walk over to the pet store?" Aunt Nora asked. "I want to look for a new water bowl for Izzie."

Nate couldn't help rolling his eyes, but he obediently followed his family down the street. Out of boredom more than anything, he began scanning the merchandise in the store windows they passed. Suddenly he gasped at the reflection of a passing vehicle. He spun around to see a Frederick's Frozen Foods truck pull up and park by

Mike's Hardware. Sam and Angelo got out of the truck and entered the store.

"Aunt Nora, can I go to Mike's for a minute?" he asked.

"Honey, it's may, not can. Yes, you may. Uncle Nick will come get you when we're done."

He nodded, crossed the street, and darted into the store, peering down each aisle to locate the duo. He found them in the nuts and bolts section. Walking past them, he knelt down and picked up a package of rope, pretending to read its label.

"These screws look sturdy enough to do the trick. What do you think?" Sam asked Angelo.

"Yeah. Reinforcing the cages is a good idea. Don't want the cargo to escape."

"Hey, lower your voice. You want everyone to know what we're doing?"

"Sorry. Yeah, they're good."

"Okay, c'mon," replied Sam.

Nate felt a hand on his shoulder and looked up.

"Hey kid. Can you hand me two packages of rope like the kind you're holding?" Angelo asked.

He gave the thug the pack he had in his hand and another from the pile on the shelf.

"Thanks, kid." Nate noticed a blood-soaked bandage wrapped around Angelo's left arm. Crimson droplets began to fall from the dressing, landing only inches away from Nate's knee.

"That's one mega cut you have on your arm," Nate remarked. "How did you do that?"

"Oh, my kitty cat scratched me," replied Angelo, as the two goons smirked at each other.

Nate just gawked at them, speechless.

"Hey kid, you might want to close your mouth. You don't want any bugs flying into it," Angelo said, giving him a wink.

They walked to the register and checked out.

"Man, what a jerk. I can't wait for the opportunity to knock that gold tooth from his big fat mouth," muttered Nate.

Outside the store, he saw his uncle waving. He ran across the street and jumped in the back of their pickup for the ride home. The frozen foods truck was long gone.

Nate gobbled his lunch and excused himself to retreat to the comfort of his bedroom. He needed to fine-tune his plan. His top priority was rescuing the teens. He needed to get them out safely. The language barrier was an issue, but he didn't think the teens would beg for an explanation. They were smart enough to realize they were up a creek without a paddle. He'd try a rescue attempt tonight; if it didn't work, he'd have Monday as backup.

The second biggest issue was the escape route. He wanted to get them out of the dungeon and off the property as quickly as possible. He kicked around three ideas in his head, finally deciding on his last one. Less risky than the other two, it was quick and convenient.

Nate would use the secret tunnel. He still needed to obtain keys from the console, but didn't anticipate a problem. He thought he would have time to rescue the teens when one of the men checked on the animals and the other remained at the console. He estimated rounds lasted thirty to forty minutes. The guy at the console could easily be distracted. It was an old building with lots of noises and probably had a century of ghost stories associated with it. Getting the hoodlum away from the desk would be simple.

This course had other advantages. Its location put them close to the cemetery and his path. As far as Nate could tell, the trap door's existence was known only to him. Everyone in this organization was focused on their illegal activities. He doubted a thorough search of the area had ever been made. The ring hidden in the dirt strengthened this conviction. The "freedom door" was twelve feet from the cell doors -- and he was the only one that knew it was there.

"Sweet...real sweet. It's like taking candy from a baby," thought Nate as he placed another check mark under the completion column of his list.

Nate's instincts told him the voice in the woods was a friend, not foe, and his gut was seldom wrong. The unknown individual hadn't lunged at him. He didn't alert the others about Nate's presence, and he didn't pursue Nate down the path. Whoever it was, he wanted his identity to remain a secret. Nate could have kicked himself from running away from this person. A friend would have been helpful. He blamed his "flight vs. fight" response on the heat of the moment and his adrenaline rush. He hoped his compatriot would be there for him this evening.

Tonight, he would borrow Uncle Nick's cell phone and alert the authorities when the group was in the tunnel. The state police had jurisdiction in this area. The closest police barracks was located on Route 36, five miles out of town. The Sheriff's Office was right in the borough. He figured that if the "staties" needed reinforcements, they'd receive assistance from neighboring police agencies. The police would figure the whole mess out once the dust settled. The cell phone guaranteed immediate assistance with the input of three little numbers.

"Cross your t's and dot your i's, and then check it again," whispered a familiar voice in his ear.

"Okay, Eric. I will," murmured a sleeping Nate.

"Good luck, stinker. I'll be watching," replied his brother.

Billy the Kid was by his side when Nate awoke from his nap. It was time to pack his knapsack. He turned it upside down, dropping its contents on his bed. This trip would be different than his previous ones. It required an array of special items. He headed downstairs for his stash, returning with an armload of loot. Opening the bag, he placed bottles of water in the bottom. The next layer consisted of fruit, Aunt Nora's homemade rice-crispy treats, and a handful of sandwiches. The snacks were cushioned by five long-sleeve flannel shirts. He placed four of the seven household flashlights on top of the shirts, stuffed extra batteries down the inside of his bag and packed rolled up socks into the side pockets on the bag's exterior. A sheathed hunting knife was squeezed between the socks.

Into his pocket Nate slipped a book of matches and a mini-flashlight. He loaded a plastic shopping bag with flip-flops and sandals, tying it to the exterior of the pack. Two giant rubber bands made the plastic bag more manageable by making it hug the backpack. He zipped the backpack shut and lifted it. It was heavier than usual but nothing he couldn't manage. Everything was prepared for tonight's rescue.

Aunt Nora called him for dinner. He placed the bag behind his bedroom door and went to his desk. He scribbled "DON'T FORGET PHONE" on a piece of paper and placed the note atop his backpack.

"Nate, did you get lost up there?" Uncle Nick called up the stairs.

"Coming!" Charging downstairs, Nate forgot to shut the door behind him.

Another storm was brewing outside. The kitchen radio reported it was going to be another doozy. Lightning flashed in the distance and thunder rumbled the hills. Nate knew the bad weather would work in his favor. It would distract the hoodlums and mask his rescue attempt.

"Nate, let's take care of the animals before all hell breaks loose," Uncle Nick said, pulling his collar up around his neck and heading for the door. Aunt Nora, who had dinner all spread out on the table, looked resigned.

Nate herded the cows and horses into their stalls, filling their troughs with apple slices. They loved their little treats. He and his uncle was heading back toward the house when two feathered messengers appeared. They landed on a fencepost and started cawing wildly.

"It's going to be a wicked storm if the crows are upset," said Uncle Nick. "I've never seen them act like that. It's like they're talking to us."

"Hmm," said Nate. He knew the creatures were there for him. He had read that depending on one's religion or culture, crows were either revered or feared; they were seen as harbingers of death, bearers of omens, or agents of healing and change. Nate's circumstances could fit any of those categories, and he wondered about the significance of a pair of birds versus just one. Personally, he distrusted crows; regardless of what their appearance meant, he couldn't get over the feeling that it didn't signify anything good. When he opened the screen door for his uncle and Max, the birds flew away, but Nate continued to stare out the window long after they left.

The fortuneteller's warning popped back into his head. "Be cautious -- your life could depend on it," she had said. Tonight, there was no room for error. He had to be playing his "A" game. Scratching his head, Nate swore that just recently, someone had given him the exact same message. But who? No one knew of his plans. He shrugged his shoulders and continued staring out into the side yard.

While Nate was reflectively gazing out the window, Billy the Kid was upstairs in Nate's room. Two things Billy loved to do were eat and snoop. The little goat had been looking for his favorite human, but since Nate wasn't there, Billy sought to avail himself of whatever munchies he could find. Uncle Nick warned Nate on several occasions not to leave stuff lying around. "Goats will eat just about anything. They're not particular," Uncle Nick had said.

Billy walked around the bed, sniffing at Nate's shoes and socks. There was nothing interesting underneath the bed. He jumped on top of it and scratched his back by rolling around the comforter. On his way out, he saw the items behind the door. He sniffed the backpack and the paper on top of it. He tried to stick his head into the bag but was unsuccessful, so he grabbed Nate's note and was munching on it when he heard his name.

"Billy! Billy! Where are you, Billy?" Nate called.

He swallowed the delicacy and ran in the direction of his master's voice.

CHAPTER 15

Windows rattled and the house shook in the grip of the high winds. Nate hoped the rain would hold off until he reached the hospital. As soon as Aunt Nora and Uncle Nick's bedroom light turned off, he crept downstairs. He rode the wind the entire way down the street. The gusts whipped Nate around like a rag doll and it required all the strength he had to keep the bike on the road. He ducked flying debris and swerved around broken tree limbs in the road, praying he wouldn't come across an airborne cow. He had to give a hand to the Erie weather team. Their prediction was once again on the money.

Nate thought of the Asian teenagers as he thrashed through the cornfield. They must be petrified. They were in a foreign land being held captive by a bunch of strangers. Their captors were barking orders to them in a language they didn't understand. They were caged like wild animals and probably fed scraps. Worst of all, they didn't know their fate. They had witnessed enough death and destruction to last their lifetime. Nobody should live like that, and Nate was determined to save them.

He was in the process of lifting up the grate when it started to rain. Quickly darting inside, he found it was difficult to move in that small space with his knapsack on his back, and dragging it across the metal tubing made too much noise. Reluctantly, Nate left the knapsack at the split in the duct and crawled to the dock grill.

Two guys were sitting at the console listening to the radio, drinking beer, and eating hamburgers. One cursed the other for winning the card game. The lightning and thunder intensified as the eye of the storm neared.

"Freaking storm. I hope it's over soon," complained one of the captors.

"It will be. Joe, hand me another beer and deal the cards," said the other. "We can get a few more hands in before we have to check on the animals."

"Yeah, yeah. Keep your shirt on," replied Joe as he shuffled the deck. "No one with a lick of sense would be out tonight. Except the boss. You know *he'll* be checking up on us."

"Yup, I figured that. He's a freaking idiot. It's a monsoon outside and he's got to be snooping around like a dog in heat. He's a piece of work, that one."

"Lou, lower your voice. That guy knows everything that's said or done around here. He probably has bugs everywhere," said Joe as he cut the deck.

"Yeah, yeah. Just keep dealing, moron. Prepare to get your nads stomped on," growled Lou.

"Those guys are real turd-sniffers," murmured Nate as he made his way through the duct to the dungeon's grill.

"Psss. Psss," whispered Nate through the opening. "Up here!"

The boy in the brown clothes had been tampering with the cell's lock, trying to jimmy it with something he found lying on the floor. The others were asleep on the mattresses.

Nate tried again. "Psss. Psss."

This time the youth heard him and scanned the room, trying to locate the source of the voice. Nate loosened the grill's screws from the inside and began to rattle the metal grate. Gripping it firmly, he pushed it forward. The bolts fell on the floor by the boy's feet, and he looked up.

Nate turned the screen around, pulled it through the opening, and laid it off to the side. Poking his head through the hole, he brought his forefinger to his lips. The boy nodded his head and turned around to make sure no one was coming.

"I know you don't understand me but I'm here to help you. I'm going to get you and the others out of here," whispered Nate to the youth.

The boy continued to stare at him.

"I wish you spoke English," Nate went on. "It would make it so much easier. Me -- friend. Here to help. Friend -- here to help."

"Thanks and we appreciate it," the boy said. "I must tell you, though, that you look pretty funny with your head sticking out from the wall like that. You look like a trophy over someone's fireplace."

Nate's eyes widened.

"You speak English. Where did you learn it?" Nate asked.

"From missionaries that came to our village. My sister, on the other side, speaks it even better than I do."

"Good. That's good. The name is Nathan Thompson. My friends call me Nate."

"Then I shall do the same. My name is Chen Wong."

"Chen, where you from?"

106

"China. The Manchurian province. We lived in a small village on the outskirts of Hailar." Seeing Nate's clueless look, the boy smiled. "It is a northern province. It borders Mongolia and southern Russia. It is near the Gobi Desert."

"Wow. You're a long way from home. I'd say welcome but considering the circumstances I'll keep my mouth shut. Hey, that was pretty fancy footwork back there. When you jumped that guy!"

"You saw that! How did you --?" Chen smiled. "Oh, your tunnel."

"Yeah, this is my home away from home," replied Nate. "I plan on redecorating it. Hang some pictures, paint it a little. Give it that homey feeling."

They looked at each other and grinned.

"Chen, I overheard them talk and they're going to sell you as slaves. I don't know to whom, or when, or where. I only know that's their plan. How about we piss them off and get you and the others out of here?"

"That sounds good to me. The sooner the better. I'm worried about the girls, especially my sister. I don't want anything happening to them."

"I don't either. Try not to worry. I'll do the best I can. Chen, here's the game plan." Nate explained his entire escape scheme to his new colleague.

"That's wonderful, my friend. How are you going to distract the second man?" Chen asked. "The one that stays at the -- I think you called it a console?"

"I don't know. I'll have to play it by ear."

"You're going to do what with your ear?"

"Going to play it by ear," repeated Nate.

Chen looked confused.

"It means taking advantage of an opportunity when it presents itself," replied Nate.

"Oh, I see."

"Chen, hang in there and be patient. It may take awhile but I'll be back. I have to wait for that opportunity. Could you do me a favor and get rid of those screws?"

"Okay, my friend. Done." Chen picked them up and buried them in the corner of the room. "Thanks for helping us. I was afraid our time had come."

"Not if I can help it," Nate said. "That's what friends are for."

They smiled at each other. The grill held tight as Nate reinserted it back into its opening.

Nate's next move was to strategically place himself near the keys. He grabbed his knapsack on the way out and although the journey was wet and soggy, he returned to the first floor, and came down the dumbwaiter. He hid behind stacked equipment in the hallway, within earshot and sight of the watchmen. He silently waited -- and waited.

"It's time to check on the animals." Joe's voice startled Nate out of his reverie.

"It's one o'clock already?" his associate asked, letting out a noisy yawn.

"Yeah. Time flies when you're having fun. Storm hasn't let up. Man, you were out like a light."

"Needed the nap. All this fresh air and greenery tires us city boys out. My system is used to pavement and exhaust fumes."

"I hear ya. Why would anyone want to live in such a godforsaken place? There are too many flies, trees, and worst -- nothing to do. This hillbilly life isn't for me, at least not yet."

"Okay, Jethro," Lou chuckled. "If you need me just holler. The radio will be strapped to my side. Be back in half an hour." He grabbed his raincoat, putting it on as he headed to the door.

"Don't drown in the rain," laughed Joe.

"Kiss this." Lou pointed to his derriére.

Joe threw an empty can at him as he exited the side door. It hit the side of the wall. Nate was alone with Joe, although Joe didn't know it. A few minutes elapsed when suddenly a clap of thunder rocked the building. The lights flickered and then went out. They were in total darkness. Nate raised his head and looked at the ceiling.

"Thank you, God," he said silently.

"Lou! Lou! Come in, Lou," yelled Joe into his walkie-talkie. "Freaking storm!"

"This is Lou. Whatcha need?"

"Lights are out. You need to come back. I've gotta check the circuit breaker."

"I don't even know where the circuit breaker is. Do you?"

"Down the hall. I'm heading there now. Monitor the console when you get here," ordered Joe.

"10-4. Rain is heavy. Gotta take it slow. I'll be there shortly."

"Okay. See you soon."

Nate's eyes adjusted to the darkness and he spotted a light coming his way. He hunched closer to the ground, concealing himself as best he could. He shut his eyes and prayed to be invisible.

"Please. Please. Let him go by," whispered Nate. When he reopened his eyes, the light was past him.

It was now or never. He slipped quietly from his hiding spot and sprinted across the trap door. As he did this, he hid his knapsack in the corner, adjacent to the trap door. He climbed the stairs and headed toward the console and the spot where the keys should be.

Bingo. They were there. He grabbed and pulled the key ring off the nail. They jiggled loudly.

"Crap," he said as he tightened his grip around them. He had just started down the stairs when the side door opened. He hid behind the trash can.

"Hey, Joe. I'm back. Where are you?" Lou yelled.

"Down the hallway."

Nate saw a flicker of light wavering down the corridor into the dock area.

"Everything all right?"

"Yeah. Just having a freaking time locating the box. I know it's around here somewhere."

"Need a hand?" Lou asked.

"Nah. I'll be all right. Stay up there."

"Gonna hit the john. Then I'll go upstairs. Holler if you need me."

"Will do."

Suddenly Nate smelled banana. He spotted a half-eaten one on top of the console. "I'll fix'em. Give them something to complain about," he said, letting out a mischievous snicker.

He separated the peel from the fruit and set them on two different steps.

"Hope they break their butts."

He darted underneath the stairwell just in the nick of time. He felt the steps vibrate as Lou climbed them.

"Son of a --!" yelled Lou, grabbing at the rail to help break his fall. He then sat down heavily on the steps to scrape the unknown substance off his shoe.

Nate grinned as he hugged the wall and slowly inched his way toward the corridor. The thunder crashed as he rounded the corner. He grabbed his backpack and ran toward the trap door. He pulled it open just a hair. It creaked and he immediately closed it, afraid the noise would expose his plans. He needed to get down there before the lights were turned on.

He waited for the next clap of thunder, which was deafening and long. He took advantage of this good fortune and opened the door. He threw his bag down the stairs and shut the door as he made his way down them in total darkness. Nate grabbed the sides of the stone wall and used them to guide him down. He was almost to the bottom when he stepped on something. It squeaked, startling him. He lost his balance, tumbling down the last two steps. He landed on the dirt floor on top of the object. He raised his hand to hit the thing but it scurried away.

"Payback is a killer," murmured Nate, thinking of his banana escapade.

He retrieved the tiny flashlight from his pocket. Its beam was faint, but gave him enough light to see.

"Chen. Chen," whispered Nate as he headed in the direction of the cell.

"Nate. I'm over here. Keep walking. You're almost here."

He saw the metal keyhole and looked up. Chen was staring at him, a wide grin on his face.

"Good work, my friend. You did it."

"We're not there yet. Pray one of these keys fit. Then you can show me on my uncle's globe where exactly you're from."

"You've got a deal."

Nate looked at the other faces peering out. They looked excited and hopeful, not whipped and defeated as before. He had to get them out. He had to!

There was only one key on the ring that looked like it would unlock the doors. He inserted and turned it.

CHAPTER 16

The internal cylinder of the lock clicked. The key made a full rotation and the door swung open. The boys ran out jumping and chattering, overjoyed they were free from captivity. They patted Nate on his back and all tried to shake his hand at once.

"Chen, I'm just as happy as your friends but tell them to pipe down. We need to be quiet."

"Yes, you're right."

Chen gathered them in a circle and talked to them. They fell mute. Nate turned his attention to the girls' door. He inserted the key and tried to turn it. It wouldn't budge. He tried it again. Still nothing. He removed it from the keyhole and wiped it clean. He tried it once more after reinserting it. Nothing. Nate kicked the cell door out of frustration and anger.

"My friend, calm down. Let me try," said Chen as he took the keys from Nate's hand.

Chen inserted the key and wiggled it, pushing the door forward, backward, hitching it up and down. The key turned and the door opened. Nate and Chen looked at each other.

"Son of a gun. How'd you do that?" Nate asked.

"It's all in the jiggle," replied Chen.

The pretty girl ran into Chen's arms. After a moment, he pulled away and turned her toward Nate.

"Let me introduce you to my sister. Nate, this is An. An, this is Nate."

She placed her palms together and then bowed from her waist.

"What does that mean?" whispered Nate to Chen.

"It's a greeting. Chinese-style."

Nate bowed back, American-style.

"Thank you for helping us," An said. "We appreciate everything you've done. I can't begin to put it into words."

"You're welcome," replied Nate. He turned toward Chen. "I would love to stay here and chat but we need to get going."

"Yes, you're right."

Nate locked the two cell doors. Their good fortune changed when the lights flickered and snapped back on. He scurried everyone away from the cameras. The hoodlums' voices echoed nearby.

"Joe. You got the keys? They're not on the nail," called Lou.

"Nah, not me. They should be underneath the console, where I left them," Joe shouted from the corridor.

"Well, they're not there."

"C'mon -- they've got to be. Look on the floor. Maybe they fell off."

"Nope. Not there."

"I'll be there in a second. Hang on."

Nate guided the group to the brick wall. He lifted up on the ring and the trap door opened.

"Hurry, everyone. Hurry. Gotta move fast," said Nate. He handed his flashlight to one of the boys and then pushed him through the opening. He pulled up on the ring once everyone was safely on the other side. He quickly patted dirt on the hoop and followed the group. The door closed. He heard the trap door open. He put his finger to his lips to quiet everyone.

"Son of a --! Joe, they're gone! Every last one of them. The cell doors are locked but they're all gone! The freaking little brats. We need to call everyone!"

"Chen, we've got to get out of here and quick," whispered a panicked Nate.

He opened his backpack and handed the additional flashlights to the others, dividing the shirts and shoes among the youths. Running to the torches on the wall, he tried to light them with the matches in his pocket. Two out of the six started burning and he handed those off. Chen turned over a bed and yanked a leg off it. Nate looked puzzled.

"Weapons, my friend. We may need weapons."

"Then you're going to love this," he replied, grabbing the sheath containing the hunting knife from his backpack and throwing it to him.

Chen pulled the knife from its cover. "Nice. Very nice."

"Don't worry. Got everything under control," Nate said reaching for his cell phone. He became frantic when he couldn't find it. He remembered he left it at home, shaking his head in disgust. His whole plan seemed to be falling to pieces around him.

He looked over to see An pulling an old cloth bag from under one of the beds. She was opening it when Chen whispered over to her.

"An. Take it with you. Let's get going."

She flung the satchel over her shoulder and joined the others.

"Amazing. Girls and their pocketbooks. Doesn't matter where they are. They've always got to have one of those things to drag around," commented Nate as he approached the tunnel. "Chen, tell your friends to shine their lights low to the ground. Don't shine them in the air. There are tree roots dangling from the ceiling. If something hits them in the face, that's probably what it is. Tell them to keep going -- don't stop for anything."

"Got it," nodded Chen.

Nate started down the tunnel. Chen agreed to be the last one in line. He made an ominous adversary with a flashlight in one hand and a knife in the other.

The storm made the stream swell. The puddle Nate had waded through before was close to a foot high. Water was seeping through the walls and ceilings. The ground was saturated. The group's progress was slow, but their spirits were soaring.

They were at the halfway mark when their secret doorway was discovered. Nate saw flashlights in the distance and heard men yelling. He and Chen switched positions so Nate could monitor their pursuers' progress. He yelled encouragement to the group, hoping to speed them up. They trudged onward and a short time later exited the tunnel.

The downpour had changed to a fine mist. Nate saw vehicle lights and herded everyone into the woods. A truck with mounted spotlights drove slowly down the road. Sounds of a two-way radio could be heard from the vehicle.

"Chen, we gotta get going. Come on. This way."

Everyone rallied behind Nate. They followed him to the cemetery road, remaining in single file and in the wood's shadow. A dog was heard in the distance and Nate knew the hound had detected their scent. He saw headstones up ahead and picked up the pace.

He looked over his shoulder to relay the good news to the rest of the group. They looked exhausted. He was pushing them to their breaking point. Several were stumbling; others put their arms around the weaker ones to help carry them. Nate didn't like the idea of resting but knew they couldn't go on like this. A few minutes of relaxation would be good for everyone, including himself.

"Chen. We'll take a break on the other side of the cemetery. It'll give the group a chance to catch their breath and get their second wind."

"Thanks for the kind gesture," remarked Chen. "But I don't think it's a smart idea. They're too close on our tails to stop. We've gotta keep on moving, no matter what."

"Are you sure?" Nate asked.

"Yes. We'll be fine. Let's keep going. I don't want to end up back in that dungeon."

"Okay," remarked Nate as they passed three freshly dug graves.

Fog was rolling in but that didn't stop the group from seeing approaching headlights. They quickened their pace and soon were thrashing and scrambling down Nate's path.

Nate tossed his knapsack into a bush -- it just slowed him down -- and stripped the trees and shrubs of their orange markers along the way.

"Why make it easy for the jerks?" Nate thought.

Freedom. He smelled freedom. He breathed a sigh of relief as the last captive crawled underneath the fence. The hard part was over. It was easy street from here on in.

Nate retrieved his bike from his hiding spot. Suddenly he heard rustling sounds and movement in the cornfield. Figures and lights became visible. Nate grabbed An by her arm and whispered, "An. Do you know how to ride a bike?"

"Yes. But why?"

"Don't ask questions. Listen to me. Take my bike. Follow the fence line. It will lead to a road. Make a right onto it. If you have to hide there's a gully on the left side of the road. You can jump down into it. Get help and make it fast. My house is the first one on the left after you pass the FOREST STATE HOSPITAL sign. The porch light is always on. Bang on the door. Wake up my aunt and uncle. Tell them what's happening and get the police."

"But --" said An, but Nate cut her off.

"Just go. NOW. Get help."

An grabbed the bike and started down the fence line.

"Nate. Where's my sister going?"

"Hopefully, to get help."

He was about to explain when Superintendent Nelson and six of his henchmen emerged from the cornfield. Chen and Nate looked at each other. Nelson had a wide grin on his face. After a considerable amount of thrashing, a team of thugs appeared on the other side of the fence. The boys scanned the entire group. Superintendent Nelson was the only one armed.

"Boys, boys, boys. I know what you're thinking. Do I run up or down the fence line? What to do, what to do?"

He started to chuckle.

"Well, you see, it doesn't matter. You can't outrun a bullet!" His sinister laughed intensified, then stopped. He looked over at his accomplices.

"Joe, Lou, get over here. Don't take all day!"

They did as he requested. They stood in front of him with their heads down, knowing they were in deep trouble.

"Why must I put up with such incompetence? I asked you to do two simple things. Keep your eyes and ears open. What was it? The beer? The idea that nothing could happen on a stormy night? Fellas, you let me down. I guess you can't let a boy do a man's job."

"Boss, we're sorry. It won't happen again. I swear!" pleaded Joe.

"You're right. It won't happen again." Nelson said lifting the gun, disengaging its safety, and pointing it at Lou's head.

"Please, boss. Have a heart. It'll never happen again. I swear. Just like Joe said," Lou choked out. He closed his eyes and waited for Nelson to pull the trigger.

"What do I know?" remarked Nelson. "I'm just a dog in heat! Lou, isn't that right?"

There was dead silence.

All of a sudden the hospital's warning siren rang, indicating another patient had walked off from the facility.

"Can things get any worse?" said Nelson turning to Sam. "I have to go to the hospital and see what's happening."

Sam nodded his head in compliance.

"Boys, this must be your lucky day," said Nelson to his two accomplices standing before him. "Oh, I'm tempted to put a bullet in each of your skulls. Really I am. If I didn't have so much on my plate you'd be goners. You know, make that your butts. I'd love to bust a cap in each of your butts because that is where your brains are. But consider this a reprieve." He turned toward Sam. "Keep a close eye on these two. I want to know if they screw up again, even just a little."

"You got it."

Nate heard Lou and Joe breathe a sigh of relief. Nelson refocused on the terrified teenagers. He pointed his weapon at them.

"It's time to deal with the troublemakers of this group." He started to scan the group starting from the far end and slowly made his way down to the two crusaders.

"Chen, my friend, I think our goose is cooked," whispered Nate as they raised their hands in the air.

"More than cooked," Chen replied, dropping his knife to the ground. "I think it's burned."

CHAPTER 17

Superintendent Nelson was right. They couldn't outrun bullets. Even if they did, they'd have the goon squad fast on their heels. No, they were trapped. Trapped like rats. Nate waited in silence for An's recapture and return to the group. Nelson began to speak.

"Well, well, well. If it isn't our little friend from up the road," said Nelson, slowly approaching Nate and lowering his gun. "Too bad it's under these circumstances. You seemed like a sharp kid. Quiet, well-behaved, well-adjusted. But I guess looks can be deceiving."

"That goes ditto for you," Nate spat out. He couldn't believe he was saying this, but he also had nothing to lose. "You're not fooling anyone with your fancy suits and shoes. What makes you think you can play God with people's lives? You're no better than these nincompoops that are doing all your dirty work for you!"

"My, oh my. Sharp tongue, quick wit, and no respect for authority," Nelson replied calmly. "What am I going to do with you?"

"Respect is a two-way street. You gotta give it before you get it. Didn't anyone teach you that? Oh, wait a minute, I forgot. You make up the rules as you go. Apparently nobody taught you anything."

Nate was primed to continue, but he was slapped across the face by the back of Nelson's hand.

"Son, you listen. I talk. It's not the other way around. Respect. It all comes down to respect."

The sting of his slap hurt but Nate refused to give his audience the satisfaction of a scream. He bit his lip as he felt the anger build up inside of him. If looks could kill, Nelson would already be dead.

Nelson turned his attentions to Chen. He walked up to the youth and stared him straight in the eye.

"Junior, I told you once before not to create trouble. But no, you wouldn't listen. Why couldn't you be like the others? Why couldn't you be a good native boy?"

Chen unexpectedly started to cough and hacked up a big goober, which he spit on Nelson's shoes. He continued to grin even after one of the goons fisted him in his stomach. Nate helped him back up from the ground.

"Respect," mused Nelson. "No one has it these days." He turned toward Sam. "These two are the problems in this pack. Get all of them back on hospital grounds. We'll meet at the dock. I'll decide what to do with them once we regroup. Gag anyone that starts yelling. I'm off to the hospital to see which patient walked off. I have my suspicions."

"Okay, boss," answered Sam.

Nelson strode toward a waiting four-wheeler and drove away. One by one the teenagers were forced to crawl under the fence and back onto the property. Their hands were retied and additional rope was placed around Chen and Nate's legs and waists. It was a precautionary measure after Chen's roundhouse kick made its mark in the groin of one of the goons.

"Man, that was a cool move!" whispered Nate to Chen when he saw the hoodlum hit the ground.

"He deserved it. It's too bad I couldn't get in a few more," replied Chen.

They were escorted single file down the path. Two thugs pulled tight on the waist ropes of the two boys, steering them slowly and awkwardly after the other captives.

"She made it," murmured a voice in his ear.

"What the --" Nate exclaimed, turning around to see who had spoken to him. He saw no one.

As they neared their destination, the hospital siren stopped. Everyone's fate started weighing heavily on Nate's mind. He was mostly worried about Chen; the others were followers. Nate knew he and Chen were the thorns in Nelson's side. He prayed that whatever punishment Nelson dished out would be swift and painless. He hoped for a stern warning but knew that was wishful thinking on his part.

He eyed Nelson and his men by the dock. He tried to walk side-by-side with Chen. He wanted to apologize for getting him into this mess. His captives pulled hard on his rope, keeping him in single file. The group was guided to the front of Nelson. He looked at them.

"Something is wrong," he remarked. "Sam, did you lose one along the way?"

"No. We didn't."

"Damn it," said Nelson, looking at Nate. "Bring him here. Right now."

Nate was dragged in front of Nelson.

"Son, I'm going to ask you once and only once. Where is the girl?"

Nate thought fast.

"I'm waiting. My patience is wearing thin."

"We left her on the path," he said. "She tripped on a rock and couldn't walk. Hurt her foot. Don't know if she sprained or broke it. We left her behind. Don't know where she went."

Nelson looked at him and then his men. "She told you she hurt her foot?" Nelson asked.

Nate knew he was being baited. "Of course not. She doesn't speak English. She made signs, motions, like she couldn't walk. She talked to the others in the group and used sign language to me."

Never taking his eyes off Nate, Nelson motioned to Sam. "Pick two or three men from the group and send them up the path. Check his story out. See if she can be found."

"You got it," replied Sam.

"Damn, she's the moneymaker of this group," lamented Nelson. "Don't take the dog. There are police in the area looking for Norman, my Houdini."

His crony nodded, chose three men, and sent them on their way. Nelson turned to face Chen and Nate.

"I guess you two are eager to learn your fate. You have a lot of spunk and gumption -- I'll give you that. There has to be someone out there looking for youngsters with all that pent-up rage. That's the best reason to let you live. On the other hand, you're schemers, conniving little escape artists. You'd be a headache to anyone that bought you. What to do? What to do? Joe, take the rest of the kids back to the dungeon. Try not to lose anyone."

Joe nodded in silence and off they went. Nelson circled the youths with his arms clasped behind him. Nate suspected that Nelson had already made his decision and was just messing with them. He was glad he busted Nelson's chops all the way to the end. Nelson stood in front of them.

"Boys, you're more trouble than you're worth," Nelson said. He turned toward Sam. "Feed them to the animals. I don't care which ones. Get rid of them."

Sam's jaw dropped as he looked at Nelson in disbelief. "The animals?"

"Did I give the order in Russian? What part of it didn't you understand? Feed them to the animals. Don't stand there looking at me like a dummy."

"Boss, they're just kids. Couldn't we just shoot them?"

"No, we just can't shoot them. I don't want any evidence lingering around that they were even here, especially the local kid. Now, I have to concentrate on finding Norman, my escape artist. I'm not happy he's on the loose somewhere out there." Nelson's eyes flickered toward the woods. "I've got to transfer that kid out of here. He's a royal pain."

Nelson walked away from the group and approached his four-wheeler. He turned around.

"Make sure the dynamic duo is alive when thrown in the cage. I want them to enjoy every moment of being ripped to shreds. All these desserts in one night. The animals are eating better than us!" Nelson chuckled as he started his four-wheeler and disappeared down the street.

The boys fought to break free but were outnumbered and outpowered. They were dragged across the road and up to the warehouse by four goons.

"You must feel like real men, killing two kids," Nate told them. "And your boss is crazy. You must know that. He's a psycho and you guys are nitwits for following him."

"Kid, it's me or you and I'm not ready to die yet," Sam replied. "I have a nice mansion and a Porsche waiting for me in the Bahamas."

"Great. Hope you wrap it around a telephone pole. If you think your house and car are going to be babe magnets, make sure you tell them how you earned it. That should impress them. What would your mother say if she knew what you were doing? Don't you have a shred of decency in you? Don't you have kids? Nephews, maybe nieces? How would you like it if one of them was going to be fed to wild animals?"

"Kid, if they talked as much as you do, I'd welcome it," answered another goon.

The others laughed. There was no room for bargaining. Their fate was sealed. The boys were lined up in front of the overhead door. One of the men flipped a switch and a few seconds later the garage door opened.

"This is it. This is how my life is going to end," thought Nate. He had one more thing to do before he died. He turned toward his friend.

"Chen, I'm sorry for getting you into this. I never thought it would get this far. If I did, I'd never have done it. I'm sorry for what's about to happen. Forgive me."

"My friend, look at me," commanded Chen.

Nate lifted his head.

"Do not apologize. You were trying to help. You risked your life for people you didn't even know. That is noble. Death will be swift. We will meet over on the other side. These cowards --" said Chen, looking at their captors, "-- they will have to answer for their mistakes somewhere down the line."

"The little turd speaks English. How about that? Come on. Let's go." Sam grabbed Chen's arm. "You first."

"No. Take me. I caused this. I should go first," insisted Nate.

"What a real hero," Sam said sarcastically. "My eyes are welling up. I think I'm going to cry. This must be one of those Kodak moments. Makes no difference to me, bucko."

He released his hold on Chen, shoving him into the clutches of another goon, who forced him to take a seat in front of the building. Suddenly Nate heard someone calling.

"Yo! Hold up!" Sam stopped and turned around. The fog was thick as pea soup and the person was unidentifiable.

"Sam, it's me. Marcel. Can't see you in all this crap. Where are you?"

"Over here, dummy. Follow my voice."

Marcel approached them.

"Nelson sent me up here to make sure things are done right. I'll take it from here," said Marcel, grabbing Nate.

"I don't need a babysitter," Sam said. "Why don't you go back down and do some more keister-kissing? You're good at that."

Marcel chuckled. "Can't do that, man. Can't do that. If you want, I'll throw the kid in. Any particular animal? Point me in that direction."

"Nah. We better do it together. Just to say it was done right, like you said."

"Are you sure? I can handle this pretty little white boy by myself."

"Yeah, I'm sure," Sam said. "Let's just do it. It's getting creepy outside."

"Whatsa matter, man? Afraid of ghosts and goblins?" laughed Marcel. "Scary haunted hospital getting to you?"

"I'm not afraid of anything, jerkface. It's just -- it feels like something is about to happen."

"Something *is* about to happen. We're gonna feed a couple of kids to the tigers!"

"No, not that. You know what I mean. I got a feeling like something really *big* is going to happen."

"Now, I've heard everything. Man, you getting one of those premonitions? Extrasensory perception, ESP?" Marcel laughed.

"Yeah, I am. I sense you're an idiot," replied Sam.

"Let's get going, fool," returned Marcel. "Boss wants us back down as soon as possible."

Nate hollered as the two men dragged him further into the building, debating whose morsel he'd become.

CHAPTER 18

Nate kicked all the way back to the rear of the building where the animals were kept. Marcel and Sam's attempts to quell his screams failed when Nate started biting any hand placed across his mouth.

The animals were housed in huge circus-type pens, enclosed on three sides. Their handlers were protected by metal bars that ran down the front, much like those of the dungeon. Latched doors on the top of each cage allowed fresh meat to be dropped in without endangering the handlers, and the opening was accessed by a ladder running up the back of the cage.

"Let's feed the little brat to the hairy brown pig," Sam suggested. "That might actually be more fun than a tiger. Takes longer."

Nate looked inside the cage just as the wild boar stuck its snout between the bars. It snorted and let out a high-pitched squeal. Nate caught a glimpse of razor-sharp teeth.

"Look, the little guy is hungry. I hope you're good and chewy. He has quite the appetite," snickered Sam.

Nate flailed back and forth. He wasn't going down without a fight. He was going to make it rough for his captors. He kicked, bit, and cursed. Marcel let loose of him to soothe an ankle that Nate kicked. And as Sam hoisted him toward the ladder, Nate grabbed one of Sam's ears in his teeth.

"You little --! Let go before I kill you myself," Sam yelled.

Sam released his hold on him and for a second Nate didn't realize his good fortune. He ran toward the front of the building, the two thugs in hot pursuit. Marcel grabbed him by his shirt. The hold made him spin around to the front of one of the lion cages. Blood-soaked material lay on its floor and he recognized it as the shirt belonging to the whip man. Bits and pieces of meat clung to the torn garment and blood splattered the cage walls. The lion growled and swiped at them, his mane matted with blood.

"You're not going anywhere, champ," Marcel told him. "Nice try. Almost made it, though, didn't you? I should kick your lily-white butt all over the place, but you'll get yours soon enough."

"Hallelujah to that," Sam agreed, rubbing his sore and bleeding ear. "It's going to be a pleasure throwing you in that cage. You've been nothing but a pain in my side since we've met."

"I second that motion," added Marcel.

"Okay, losers," Nate snapped back. "Whatever you say. I'm sure you guys and the other douche bags will meet up in Hell."

"You just can't keep that trap shut, can you?" Sam yelled, raising an arm to backhand him.

"Easy, Sam. Easy," Marcel said. "He's playing you. He's pushing your buttons and you're falling for it. Come on, little man."

Marcel pushed, pulled, and dragged Nate back to the rear of the cage.

"You're right. The little jerk is screwing with me!" Sam pushed

Marcel out of the way. "I'm going to teach the little brat one last lesson before he goes bye-bye."

He raised his arm again and brought it forward with all his strength. Before he could make contact with Nate, however, Sam lost his footing in a puddle and fell to the ground. He rolled around on the wet floor, trying to get up. Nate realized the liquid was animal urine and cracked up.

"Hey, stinky. Serves you right," laughed Nate. "Ooh, I've fallen but I don't want to get up. I love rolling around in animal pee!"

Marcel snickered, becoming serious when he realized Nate was watching him.

"Quit screwing around," Marcel said firmly. "Let's get this over with."

"My pleasure," said a frustrated Sam, getting up and wiping himself off as best he could.

The very same rope that Nate had handed Sam and Angelo in Mike's store that morning was now used to bind his arms to his body. Even bound, however, Nate was not ready to give in; it took both Marcel and Sam to hoist him on top of the animal cage.

"Let me open the trap door. We'll throw him in. Rope and all."

Sam knelt down and opened the metal cover.

"Bring him here," yelled Sam.

Nate closed his eyes and began to pray. Tears streamed down his face. This was it. The end. His last purpose in life was as animal food. His anxiety was replaced by calm surprise as he realized he was no longer scared. He'd accepted his fate and was ready to meet his Maker. He hoped his parents and brother would be over on the other side to greet him. Then he heard the words.

"New York City Police. You're under arrest."

He opened his eyes. Marcel had let go of him and was standing on top of the cage with his badge out and his gun drawn. Pocketing the badge, he pulled Nate behind him, away from the hole and Sam.

"I should have known. Had a bad feeling about you from the start," Sam said. "Aren't you a little out of your jurisdiction, oink man?"

"Never mind the questions. Put your hands behind your head and kneel down," demanded Marcel. "We can make this go down easy or hard. It's up to you. Your decision."

"Screw you, pig. You're about to get a royal butt-whipping," Sam retorted.

"Bring it on. What did the kid say? Oh, yeah. Bring it on, stinky."

Sam jumped over the opening and onto Marcel. The 9mm went flying and landed on the other side of the cage. Nate ran and tried to pick it up but couldn't, so he kicked it off the cage, hoping it wouldn't discharge when it hit the ground. It didn't. Marcel wrestled Sam down onto the flat roof. Nate decided to assist his savior and waited for the chance to present itself. Just as it came, they reversed positions and Nate accidentally kicked Marcel in the head.

"Hey kid. I'm trying to help you. Enough of the fancy footwork," Marcel told him, grabbing Sam by his collar and dishing him a few face-fists.

"Had enough? Want more?" Marcel asked as he turned the goon on his stomach. "Man, you smell bad. Worse than the last hooker I arrested."

"You good-for-nothing Oreo," yelled Sam, trying to push Marcel off him.

"No. You just didn't say that. This is the time to try to get on my good side, not my bad!"

"What are you going to do? Turn me over to the Justice Department, Uncle Tom?"

"You're hurting my feelings," Marcel said. "Now you should apologize. It's not nice to hate other races. Can't we all just get along?"

Suddenly, inexplicably, Sam was on his feet. Marcel and Nate froze as he began to back across the top of the cage and reach for something inside his jacket. One second he was there and the next he was gone. Marcel lunged to grab him but it was too late. Sam fell through the hole into the cage.

The bloodcurdling screams didn't last long. The boar went wild over the fresh meat. Nate walked over to the opening and tried to look in, but Marcel blocked his path.

"Kid, you don't want to do that," Marcel said, closing the door. "Let's get you out of that mummy outfit."

He removed the rope binding Nate.

"Thank you *so much.* I thought I was a goner." Nate's emotions let loose and he threw his arms around the cop.

"It's okay, kid. It's okay. Everything is gonna be all right," said Marcel, patting him on the back.

Nate let go and looked at him.

"My friend. Chen. What about my friend?"

"Let's get him," said the cop, pointing toward the ladder. "Hold up for a second," he said, pulling a cell phone from his pants pocket. Dialing a number, he turned away and started talking. At last he nodded his head. "Right. Right. Got it."

They started to climb down the ladder, Marcel first. The cop was on the last rung when someone grabbed him from the side and flung him headlong across the room. Nate jumped the last remaining rungs to charge Marcel's assailant.

The gigantic figure stood over Marcel, looking down at him. Momentarily disoriented, Marcel finally opened his eyes.

"Man, oh man. You are one ugly mother," he blurted out.

The huge man hoisted Marcel into the air with his left arm and curled his right hand into a fist. Marcel was about to get pulverized when he heard Nate yell.

"Ralph. Ralph. Don't do it! Don't do it! He's a good guy. He's a cop. He's here to help."

Ralph lowered his fist, and Nate grabbed it.

"Honest. Ralph, he's okay. He saved my life."

Ralph released his hold on Marcel, and the smaller man dropped to the floor.

"Whoa there, partner," Marcel gasped. "You have one mega grip. You're strong as an ox. Glad you're on our side. Say man, didn't mean that 'ugly mother' remark. Just kidding!"

Ralph offered a hand to help Marcel to his feet. Marcel slapped Ralph's back and readjusted the big man's disheveled shirt.

"Guys. We gotta get the others," begged Nate.

"I need my gun," Marcel said, looking around.

"I know where it is!" Nate told him. He spotted it right where his foot had sent it -- lying next to the wall in a clump of dirt.

"Come here, my precious little girl. Daddy loves you so much!" Marcel wiped off his weapon and kissed it before replacing it in his holster. "We'll give you a good cleaning once this is all done."

Ralph and Nate looked at one another.

"Me and the old girl have been through a lot. She's the first gun I've ever owned and -- knock on wood -- the last one I'll ever need."

Nate shrugged his shoulders. "Who was he to judge? His best friend was a goat."

They sneaked up to the front of the building and eyed their opposition. Chen was sitting on the ground in front of the three remaining men. Their backs were turned away from the building.

Ralph tapped Marcel on the shoulder, pointing to the two biggest men. He indicated they were his. Marcel would get the remaining crook.

"I wonder what's taking them so long. How hard is it to dump a bratty kid into a cage?" one of them remarked.

"The kid's probably trying to talk them out of it. Relax. It'll all be over soon," replied another, taking a drag from his cigarette.

They never saw it coming. Ralph lifted two of the goons in the air and shook them until they were too dizzy to stand. Marcel applied a choke hold to his and slowly lowered him to the ground where he was then handcuffed. Marcel pulled flexi-cuffs from inside his jacket and handed them to Ralph, who trussed up his two victims.

Nate ran to his friend and untied him, pulling him to his feet. They looked at each other, smiled, and embraced. Chen suddenly caught sight of Ralph and his jaw dropped.

"Wow, you grow them big in your country!"

Everyone laughed. Marcel pulled the phone from his pocket and made another call.

"The cavalry is coming. Hang tight. They'll be arriving shortly."

Nate was the first to hear the helicopters. He couldn't see them but it was a relief to know they were there. The fog slowly lifted, revealing the beginning of an all-out assault on the hospital grounds. Men in police gear were repelling from choppers. The flying birds dropped them everywhere around the old sanitarium. A procession of police vehicles streamed onto the grounds, splitting up in different directions to surround the entire structure. Marcel pulled out his badge and secured it around his neck with a chain.

"Guys, give them time," he advised. "Let them get situated. We'll hold the fort up here for a few minutes."

"Cool. Pretty cool," said Nate, turning to Chen.

"You're right. Pretty cool."

"Chen, welcome to America."

"Thank you. It's been an interesting journey."

The boys squatted on the ground and watched the action.

CHAPTER 19

The hoodlums ran in every direction trying to escape custody. But one by one they were arrested, handcuffed, and brought to a make-shift jail set up by the docks.

A four-man swat team jogged up to Nate's group.

"Hey Mar, you old dog!" the leader called out cheerfully. "How come I always have to save your sorry butt? Don't you have better things to do on a Sunday night?"

"Sure do. Your sister's at home waiting for me."

Grinning, they clasped hands in a show of camaraderie.

"What's with the 'do?" the team leader asked. "You look like something the cat dragged in!"

"My undercover garb. Trying to look like a scumbag," returned Marcel.

"Yeah, well, you do. Here, put this on," the team leader said, handing Marcel a vest marked POLICE.

"There are a lot of people and agencies here that don't know you.

This will give them a clue which team you're on. Wouldn't want you to end up in the slammer, although the boss would probably get a good laugh out of it."

"Yeah, he probably would. Thanks, bro."

The squad leader turned and looked at Ralph.

"Man, oh man. You must have eaten your Wheaties when you were a kid, and then some!" the officer said in awe. "Here, Tiny. Try this on for size."

He handed Ralph another vest. The officer turned back to Marcel but not before noticing Nate and Chen. "Well, what do we have here?" he asked.

"Our replacements," remarked Marcel. "These two remind me of us in our younger days. Always in the thick of things."

He was about to speak when someone began yelling.

"Let go of me. Let go of me. Let go, you jerk!"

Norm appeared around the side of the warehouse with one of Nelson's goons dangling from his armpit, the hoodlum held firmly in a headlock.

"Found girl on road," Norm explained. "Took her to house. She told us what happened. Wanted to help. Norm wanted to help."

"You did, Norman. And you did a great job," Ralph assured him. "Now, let him go so the police can take him."

Norm complied. The team took custody of the punk and placed him with the others. Nate and Chen, mesmerized by all the action, followed the police and their prisoners down the slope.

Two semis pulled up in front of the warehouse. Men in windbreakers jumped from the passenger side of each cab. When they turned, Nate observed the logos of the Pittsburgh and Erie zoos. The zoo representatives talked with police and headed into the building to inventory the animals they would temporarily house at their facilities.

A handcuffed Superintendent Nelson was led out of the building and placed in the back of a police cruiser. Nate made eye contact with him, placed his thumb on his nose, wagged his four fingers, and stuck his tongue out at him.

Nelson leaned forward to yell something derogatory at Nate but the officers in charge roughly pushed him back. The youth continued his harassment.

"Nate, stop taunting the zoo animal."

Nate turned around to see Marcel and another man.

"Can't you see he's getting all upset?" Marcel went on. "If you keep this up, we'll have to shoot him with a tranquilizer gun to calm him down."

Nelson shouted obscenities at Marcel, many reflecting his opinion of Marcel's skin tone and background.

"Man, oh man. What is this? Redneck capital of the Northeast? Detective, how many hillbillies do you have living up here?"

"It's hard to tell. They keep blowing themselves up in their meth labs," replied the plainclothes officer.

"I hate to say this, but better you than us. Anyhow, this is the young man I was talking to you about. If anybody can help you with your investigation, it's him."

"Thanks, Marcel. Give me just a minute, son, and I'll be right with you," the detective said to Nate.

Marcel turned to Nate. "Look, man, I just found out about your family. I lost my dad in Vietnam. Hang in there. You never get over it, but things get better. You can count on it."

Nate nodded. "Thanks for being here when we needed you."

"Anytime, kid. Anytime." He gave Nate's shoulder a squeeze and jogged off in the direction of his friend's SWAT team.

Left alone for a moment, Nate scanned the site for his friend Chen and finally located him down by a cluster of ambulances. Chen and An appeared to be translating between the EMTs, INS personnel, and the freed captives, some of whom were receiving medical attention.

The detective returned, Norm and Ralph at his side. "Hello, Nate. I'm Detective Gary Pickens. I'm with the Pennsylvania State Police. I was wondering if you'd be willing to help me in my investigation. What do you say?"

"Yes, sir. Where do you want to start?"

"At the beginning, son. At the beginning," replied the detective. "Before we get started, though, do you know anything about this bag? One of your cohorts was carrying it around."

Nate recognized it as the bag An had taken from the secret room. "Not really, sir. It was underneath one of the beds in the hidden room, adjacent to the dungeon."

The detective opened it, and withdrew a scrap of cloth that looked eerily familiar to Nate. Brown, stained, and old, it depicted eight star points around a contrasting square. "Wow! The stories are true about the old hospital. This probably dates from the Underground Railroad," the detective said. "It's the North Star -- slaves followed it to freedom. This was one of the routes they took. Let's hope the quilt's owner made it to wherever he was going."

Suddenly Nate's dream came back to him in full force -- the escape from the underground tunnel, the doomed flight from their pursuers, the crack of gunfire, his brother dying in his arms.

"He did make it," Nate blurted out. "I know he did. Unfortunately, his brother didn't. He died over there, a bullet to his neck." He pointed over to a section of the woods.

"Oo...kay. I'll take your word for it," replied Pickens.

Nate, Ralph, Norman and the detective sat on the side of the dock. Nate started to talk and left nothing out. Ralph was able to fill in many missing details, and Nate was surprised to learn that Ralph was the one who had called his name in the woods that dark and foggy night.

As the story poured out, Pickens jotted notes on a small pad. He excused himself and made a phone call. While he was gone, Marcel's uniformed friend recruited Norman and Ralph to help with the prisoners. Detective Pickens returned.

"Nate. You feel like taking a walk up to the cemetery?"

He nodded in agreement.

They had just started their journey up the road when Nate heard someone yelling behind them.

"Dad. Dad. Wait up," the unknown voice shouted.

It was Dylan, the quarterback Nate had met at school. He was wearing a PA State Police cadet jacket.

"Dad, they told me you were on the way to the cemetery. May I tag along? They've got loads of guys guarding the prisoners, and I'm getting bored."

"Sure thing, son. Nate, this is Dylan. Dylan -- Nate."

"Got that covered. We've already met," replied Dylan with a smile.

"Good. Let's get going."

They were joined by two other uniformed police officers.

As the two teens walked alongside each other, Dylan whispered over to Nate, "Hey, squirt. What in the world have you gotten yourself into?"

"Long story."

"You're going to tell me, though, right?"

"Gonna pass me the football once in a while?"

Dylan grinned. "With that arm? I think that can be arranged."

"Okay. I'll fill you in later," replied Nate.

They were almost to the entrance when they heard faint moans. The officers drew their guns.

"Everyone spread out and be careful," Pickens commanded softly. "Boys, stay with me."

He raised his voice and called out, "State police. Show yourself. Come out with your hands in the air."

The groaning continued.

"Gary, sounds like the person is hurt," said one of the other officers. "I don't think anyone would be that noisy if they were planning an ambush."

"Agreed. Let's continue the search," replied Pickens.

Everyone holstered their weapons. They continued sweeping the area, searching for the source of the sound. One of the officers pointed to a grassy patch alongside the route. Pickens cautiously approached, knelt down and started to crawl. He patted the top of the lawn, stopped, and extended his head downward to look at something.

"Casey, call for an ambulance. Get a rescue squad up here. Looks like one of the perps fell into this hole."

"Got it, boss."

A wide-eyed Nate asked Pickens if he could take a look. Pickens nodded in agreement. The culprit was lying on the dirt floor, his arms and legs bent awkwardly. The battered man whimpered but did not move. Nate sat off to the hole's side.

"Doing okay, kid?" Pickens asked.

"Yeah. I'm fine."

"He's messed up. From his position I'd say he has broken arms and legs -- possibly worse. He'd better be thankful we headed up this way. He would've died in that hole."

Nate heard little of what the police detective said. He was thinking of the other night -- the night he was frightened by Ralph's voice in the woods. He remembered the mist detouring him away from this grassy area. His guardian ghost had protected him. He made the sign of the cross across his chest and silently thanked his unknown protector.

The ambulance and rescue crew arrived and the original group continued into the cemetery.

Nate began to explain to the detective about the inconsistencies of the headstones, pointing to the three fresh graves. Pickens dragged him along as he counted and recorded the grave markers. They neared the mausoleum tucked in the woods. Nate tapped Pickens's arm and directed his attention to its roof.

"Good golly, Miss Molly," said Pickens. "That's a bat and a half! Hate them," he continued. "I had a bad experience with one when I was a kid." He picked up a rock and threw it at the creature. The bat screeched and flew away.

It wasn't long before hearses arrived on the scene. They were followed by C.S.I. units. Pickens updated the crime scene supervisor and within minutes the team pulled shovels from their vehicles and headed toward the fresh gravesites. Casey, Pickens' associate, and Dylan remained behind to monitor the operation.

Pickens called for Nate, who had wandered off and was staring down at a headstone in the back row. Along with the other uniformed officer, the trio started their walk back to the hospital. "Nate, you've got good instincts and you've sure got guts. Ever think about becoming a cop when you get older?" Pickens asked.

"Nope," Nate said firmly. "I'm going to be a stuntman. Wanna jump out of planes and fall off of buildings and drive burning cars.

You know. Neat stuff like that."

Pickens smiled at the young man. "Right."

He put his arm around Nate's shoulder and they continued down the hill.

Halfway to their destination, Nate heard the voice whisper in his ear. He looked around but knew he wouldn't see anyone.

"Stinker, your life is going to be wonderful."

A teary-eyed Nate murmured back. "But Eric, I won't be with you."

"It's all right. Our Father has sent you a replacement. Be happy."

"Okay, big brother. Will you keep talking to me, though?"

"You can count on it."

Nate smiled, wiping the tears from his cheeks.

With the number of emergency vehicles on site, the area around the hospital was lit up like an amusement park. Everywhere Nate looked, there were people. Suddenly he spotted Chen and the other youths getting into an INS van. He started toward it when all of a sudden he heard the engine catch and the brake lights flash. The vehicle pulled onto the road, heading toward the gates.

"Chen!" Nate screamed. He took off after the van. But the last thing he saw was Chen's good-bye wave from the rear window.

He hung his head in sorrow. "I'll never see him again."

"Nate! Over here!"

Nate lifted his head again, recognizing the familiar voice. Parked just outside the crime scene barricades, he saw the Bluemobile. Nate ran toward the truck and peered inside. It was empty. Someone tapped his shoulder and he turned around. Aunt Nora stood there crying, Uncle Nick stood by her side, and Nate felt the weight of the world being lifted off his shoulders. He threw himself into a group hug.

"I'm sorry I put you through all of this!" Nate blurted out. "I didn't realize how big this thing was -- and I didn't think you'd believe me if I told you."

"Son, that's probably true," his uncle said. "Who would've thought something like this could happen in our sleepy little town? But you did the right thing, all the way down the line, and we're proud of you. We couldn't ask for anything more."

"You don't hate me? For lying to you, for not telling you where I was going or what I thought was going on --?"

"Hate you?" Aunt Nora gasped. "Nate, how could you think that? We love you; you're our family."

"Always remember that," Uncle Nick said. "Now, are you ready to go home? Get an early breakfast and some shuteye?"

Nate nodded vigorously.

"Good. Tomorrow we're heading into town to see Doug Baines, the architect. It looks like we'll be putting on an addition to the house. Some of those Asian kids you rescued are going to be allowed to stay in this country if they can find foster parents, and Nora and I have decided we'd like to take a couple of them in. Okay with you?"

"Definitely," Nate agreed, wiping the tear from the corner of his eye.

"We also need to stop by Forest State Hospital," continued Uncle Nick. "I'd like to talk with someone about hiring Norm as a ranch hand. Heck, he's always at our house, might as well offer him a job!"

"Sounds good," replied Nate. "He's an okay guy."

"Yeah, you're right," said Uncle Nick, hugging him as he opened the vehicle's door. "Oh, by the way," added Uncle Nick. "You're grounded for the rest of your life."

Nate laughed. He was glad to be going home.

Epilogue

Nate scooted the dolly out from underneath the Bluemobile when he heard the lunch bell clang. Chen extended a hand and pulled him to his feet. Nate had been busy changing the truck's oil while Chen replaced the spark plugs and wires.

"Catch!" Chen tossed a plastic container of cleaning wipes at Nate. Chen himself was diligently using the wipes to smear black grease all over his face and neck. Nate restrained the urge to laugh out loud.

"Hurry up!" Chen commanded, gesturing at the wipes in Nate's hands. "Clean up -- I'm hungry as a pig!"

"Well, you kinda look like one," said Nate. He angled the driver's side mirror so Chen could see his reflection. "Oink! Oink!"

"Hey, at least I clean up well," Chen said, snatching the wipes back and trying again. "You can't say the same about that ugly mug of yours!"

Laughing, the boys chased each other out of the garage. They raced past Uncle Nick and Ralph, who looked up from the tractor and chuckled.

When Chen was twenty feet ahead of Nate, he spun around and assumed a karate stance.

"Come on, dork. Let me have it," Chen demanded.

"If you're cruising for a bruising, I'm your man," returned Nate. "Bring it on, tough guy."

Within seconds, the boys were throwing roundhouse kicks at one another.

"Guys, take it easy," warned Uncle Nick. "I don't want to spend a gorgeous day sitting in the emergency room!"

"Okay, Dad," laughed Chen. "I'll just hurt him a little."

"Chennnnn..."

Under Uncle Nick's watchful eye, the boys stopped kicking, slapped each other on the back, and continued walking toward the house. They paused, watching another tractor come to a halt by the barn.

"Hey, Norm," Nate called. "Mom promised us fried chicken and potato salad. Hurry up."

"I'm coming. Let me park this contraption and put my gloves down," Norm hollered back.

The groups made their way to the back porch, taking their usual places around the picnic table. An was tossing the salad. Max and the goats were situated on each side of her, hoping she'd drop something, anything, on the floor. Aunt Nora brought out the platter of chicken.

After everyone was seated and their heads bowed, Uncle Nick said the blessing. Everyone dug into the scrumptious meal as soon as their "amens" were said.

Nate quietly sat in his spot, eating and thinking. He had marked his one-year anniversary in Woodson two weeks ago. He thought he'd never be happy again after losing his family. Yet, here he was -- a country boy, content with his new life in what had to be the most beautiful place on earth. He remembered what Marcel, the undercover police officer, had said to him over a year ago. Marcel had been right; things did get better over time.

In the beginning, Nate had his bad days, when all he did was cry and mourn the loss of his family. Those days were eventually replaced with happy times with Aunt Nora and Uncle Nick, and as time passed, he was able to savor his joyous memories of the Thompson clan as well. The hurt slowly subsided and although he thought of his parents and brother every day, the memories no longer tormented him.

Nate adored his aunt and uncle and even though they couldn't replace his parents, they came pretty close. He remembered that the first time he referred to them as Mom and Dad, it brought tears to their eyes. "Yeah," he thought. "He couldn't have found a better home."

And he was ecstatic about having Chen and An as siblings. Chen picked up where Eric had left off. Their classmates called the two "Siamese twins," and it was true. Nate turned and looked at his brother, and Chen grinned back. There had been an instant bond between the two, stronger than the strongest of glues.

An turned out to be a tomboy and Nate was pleased he could roughhouse with her. Although she was petite and dainty, An had the best right hook he'd ever seen in a girl. Nate and Chen were already working out strategies to keep the boys away from their little sister when she started high school this coming fall -- for the boys' own good, of course! An just laughed, calling her brothers goofballs.

Nate's siblings relished the slower pace of country life, as did he. The family was close-knit and they enjoyed working alongside each other on the farm. No one minded the manual labor, dirty hands, or the occasional callus. Being together was all that mattered.

Nate's biggest surprise was how his Aunt Nora and Uncle Nick blossomed as parents. It was no surprise when Nora suggested taking in Chen and An. But it was completely miraculous to see Uncle Nick, the family rabble rouser, settle into a fatherly role. It wasn't long before he became a class chaperone, chauffeur, and vice-president of the PTA. In the process, he tamed down, became more responsible, and welcomed everyone into his family, including Norman and Ralph.

Uncle Nick protected his household, and this was never more evident than when television and newspaper reporters bombarded their house wanting personal interviews with Nate. Uncle Nick, with help from Izzie, chased numerous reporters off their property. Nate chuckled, remembering a few journalists that got the good ole Izzie "rear-end" ram.

Nate couldn't care less about becoming a celebrity. He didn't want the status or drama that went with it. He was uncomfortable with his notoriety, and couldn't understand all the hoopla for doing the right thing. The media proclaimed him a hero, but he didn't agree. He thought he had merely been at the right place at the right time, and anyone would have done what he did.

But notoriety rained down on the little family whether they asked for it or not, and with the fame came money. Gratuities secured all the children's college funds. Nate donated the rest to charity, setting up a foundation in memory of his mom, dad, and brother Eric. He contributed to a nearby wildlife sanctuary, a children's cancer center, a New Orleans neighborhood, and an organization dedicated to fighting worldwide slavery. The bulk of the rest went to help rebuild the town of Greenville after a tornado leveled the entire Oklahoma community.

"Farmers should help farmers," said a tearful Uncle Nick as he handed the check to the mayor of the small town.

Nate smiled at the memory and grabbed another piece of chicken from the platter.

The previous summer Nate discovered his psychic ability, or his sixth sense as some people called it. Nate learned to control his outbursts because they frightened people. Although his talks with Eric continued, they were becoming scarcer as Nate grew more comfortable in his new life.

Out of all the gratuities offered, Nate accepted only one. He had always wanted to go out West to attend a training camp for would-be stuntmen. After hearing his story, the camp's owners offered him an all-expense-paid summer vacation for himself and three friends. He couldn't pass up that kind of opportunity.

Visiting Henderson, Nevada would be a great adventure -- and he would get to work with real stuntmen on real movie sets! Best of all, he reasoned, he'd get a real adrenaline rush without putting anybody in mortal danger. He'd had enough of that for a while!

Blast-off for this adventure was scheduled for next week. He and his friends would be landing at McCarran International Airport next Friday.

"Yeah," Nate thought as he finished off the last bite of chicken. "This trip is going to be cooler than cool. After all -- what could possibly go wrong in the middle of a desert?"

His thoughts were interrupted by a jab in the shoulder. Nate swung around to return the favor, but Chen had already vaulted over the porch railing onto the grass below.

"Hey, chump," Chen called. "Don't you want to get in shape for next week? Betcha can't beat me to the old oak tree!"

He heard chuckling from his family members.

"Bring it on, slickster. Bring it on," Nate replied as he jumped from the porch, Billy the Kid scampering faithfully by his side.

CPSIA information can be obtained at www.ICGtesting.com
Printed in the USA
BVOW051127030912

299440BV00002B/2/P